I0721303

Stories from the Darkside

By

Colin Reardon

I would like to dedicate the book to my wife, Clare, who always made me believe that anything is possible.

Preface

When the fog of the ordinary lifts, what we often find lurking beneath is far more unsettling than we ever dared to imagine. "Stories from the Darkside" invites you to step into that fog, where the thin line between reality and the supernatural blurs into something altogether more sinister. These are tales that do not simply echo the unknown; they confront it head-on. With every turn of the page, you will find yourself entwined with characters who experience the inexplicable, the unnerving, and the downright chilling.

Every story within this book is drawn from the shadowy places we all fear to visit, but secretly long to explore. From forgotten towns to eerie historical events, these narratives pull back the curtain on a world of ghosts, lost souls, and forgotten horrors. And as you journey through these dark corners of the human psyche, one question remains: what is real, and what is merely a reflection of our deepest, most terrifying fears?

Take a step into the unknown, and be prepared. Once you enter the dark, there's no telling when you'll escape or what you might bring back with you.

Table of Contents

Chapter 1
The Watchers

Many people, as children, heard their parents or grandparents recount tales of their youth. These stories often included experiences of serving in the military during wartime, working on the home front in various capacities, and enduring food and supply rationing. They also highlighted the strong community spirit that helped them persevere through tough times, as well as the social events that offered much-needed breaks from the stresses of war. These accounts reflected survival, resilience, courage, and the ability to find moments of happiness despite adversity.

For instance, our fathers or grandfathers might recount their time as soldiers on the front lines, describing the camaraderie among the troops and the intense battles they faced. Meanwhile, our mothers or grandmothers might share memories of working in factories, producing essential goods for the war effort, tending victory gardens to ensure there was enough food, or even joining one of the many women's armed forces. Stories of standing in long lines for rations and making do with limited supplies were common, illustrating the resourcefulness people had to develop.

Community spirit played a significant role in these narratives, with neighbours helping each other repair homes damaged by bombings or sharing whatever little they had. Social events like dances, community plays, and musical performances in air-raid shelters provided welcome relief, offering a chance to laugh and enjoy life in small ways.

These personal histories not only depicted the hardships faced but also celebrated the incredible human spirit that flourished amidst such trying circumstances.

It is widely accepted that the Second World War ended in September 1945. However, the truth is that it actually ended on June 8th, 1945. Before you go verifying this online, let me introduce Emily Croft, whose story sheds light on this lesser-known fact.

During her childhood, Emily would sit on her grandfather's lap as he recounted his experiences during the war. He spoke of his rescue from Dunkirk, though he often omitted certain details, such as the sights he witnessed, the friends he lost, and how he ultimately ended up in a wheelchair.

Before becoming wheelchair-bound, Terry Gaines was a man of considerable stature, standing at six feet six inches with a robust build and ginger hair that shimmered like fire in the sunlight. His strength and presence were matched by his gentle nature and kind heart, earning him the affectionate nickname "Gentle Giant" among those who knew him well. Despite his imposing figure, he had a soft spot for children and animals, often seen playing with Emily and her friends when they visited with Emily's parents, or tending to stray cats that wandered near his home.

Initially aspiring to join the navy, he dreamt of sailing the high seas and exploring distant lands. However, his struggles with seasickness dashed these hopes, leading him to enlist in the army instead. He adapted to army life quickly, driven by a deep sense of duty and patriotism. While he rarely spoke of the horrors of war to anyone, the haunted look in his eyes when he paused between stories hinted at the deep scars left on his soul. Each retelling was a way for him to process his past, sharing only what he could bear to relive while shielding his beloved granddaughter from the harshest truths.

He lost his wife, Doris, to tuberculosis in 1938 and never remarried. Doris had been his childhood sweetheart; they lived on the same street and had been inseparable ever since. At the age of forty-five, he had offers from a few women, but he declined, feeling a strong connection to Doris.

He believed Doris would be waiting for him, sitting on a bench outside the pearly gates. He thought that meeting someone else would be a form of disloyalty. The memory of their life together—her laughter, their shared dreams, and the hardships they weathered—continued to influence his decisions and kept her alive in his heart.

As Emily grew older, she would accompany her grandfather to his local pub, The Pipe Makers Arms. He often referred to this establishment as his second home, having frequented it since he was seventeen. Now in his nineties, he still enjoyed spending a couple of hours there, engaging in conversation with the bar staff and several regular customers.

Emily cherished the time she spent with her grandfather, as he had significantly contributed to her development through guidance and by teaching her how to play the piano. She would often listen attentively to his lessons, soaking up every bit of wisdom he imparted. His hands, though aged, moved gracefully over the piano keys, producing melodies that filled the room with warmth and joy.

Although she had never met her grandmother, her grandfather would retrieve old photo albums and present black-and-white photographs to Emily, vividly describing her grandmother's appearance. Each photograph seemed to come alive with his words. He spoke of her dark brown hair cascading down like a waterfall, her hazel eyes sparkling with mischief and affection, and the most endearing smile that could light up any room. These moments, steeped in history and emotion, helped Emily form a picture of her grandmother, a woman she felt connected to despite their paths never crossing.

May 5th is a date that will remain unforgettable for Emily, as it marked a significant and painful moment in her life. On this day, her grandfather passed away, leaving her with a profound sense of loss. Although she understood the inevitability of mortality, she had deeply hoped her grandfather could have lived longer.

The days following her grandfather's passing were marked by an aching stillness in Emily's heart and the home he left behind. She found herself drawn to the flat where he spent his final years—a place that seemed steeped in quiet solitude yet vibrant with fragments of a life well-lived. Her parents encouraged her to sort through some of his belongings, hoping it might provide a sense of closure, though Emily knew it would only awaken more memories.

As she stepped inside, the air was heavy with the weight of absence. The faint ticking of a clock seemed louder than it should have been, each second amplifying the emptiness. Emily's eyes wandered across the room, settling on the fragile traces of her grandfather's routine: a pipe resting on the mantle, a pair of spectacles folded neatly on a half-finished crossword, and a jar of boiled sweets on the corner table—half-empty but still there, as though awaiting his return.

Unable to shake the feeling of loss, she began to move through the flat, her touch gentle and reverent. It was here, amidst the books, trinkets, and handwritten notes, that Emily started to rediscover the man she had loved so deeplyhis humour, his wisdom, and the quiet vulnerability he rarely showed to others. Each object she encountered seemed to echo his presence, whispering fragments of his story into her yearning soul.

The flat was silent as Emily looked at the armchair that had been her grandfather's regular seat, its worn leather indicating extensive use. The room held a faint aroma of lavender, old paper, and traces of her grandfather's cologne. Emily touched the armrest of the chair, noting the soft indentations formed over time, reflecting on the history and presence of the man who once occupied it. Tears welled up in her eyes as memories flooded back.

Emily stepped into the spare room, where sunlight streamed through the window, casting golden spots across the cluttered space. Boxes were neatly stacked in the corner, and beneath the window, in front of them, stood an old pale blue metal trunk. The room carried a faint musty odour, mixed with the scent of ageing paper. Dust particles floated in the sunbeams, lending the room a timeless feel.

She knelt before the trunk, her heart racing with curiosity and a touch of nostalgia. Opening the trunk, she discovered several old shoeboxes filled with cigarette cards, postcards, and a ration book. There were stacks of letters, a well-used Bible, and a soldier's hymn book. Each item seemed to whisper stories from the past, waiting to be revealed. The letters were tied with a faded green ribbon, their paper yellowed with age, suggesting they had been read many times over the years.

Then Emily spotted a folded newspaper cutting about her grandfather. Its brittle, yellowing edges immediately caught her attention. With careful hands, she unfolded it and began to read. The article recounted a heartbreaking incident that happened on Saturday, 15th April 1945, when he had a heated argument with Doris, stormed out of the butcher's, and tragically stepped into the path of a tram. The accident left him paralysed from the waist down.

Emily discovered this painful chapter and the profound impact it had on her grandfather's life. She had always believed that her grandfather's injuries were sustained at Dunkirk and was devastated to learn the true cause of his condition. Her sadness deepened as she read through the letters her grandmother wrote to her grandfather while he was in France, each letter filled with longing and sorrow at their separation.

After spending most of the day at her grandfather's flat, she decided to go to The Pipe Makers Arms pub and have a drink in his memory.

The moment Emily stepped through the weathered doors, she was struck by an uncanny sense of dislocation. The air thickened with the scent of tobacco and aged wood. Smoke-stained paintwork and bare floorboards stretched before her, lit by dim lights hanging from the walls. There were men in waistcoats and flat caps drinking pints, and a few women sitting at tables drinking from small glasses. The pub was filled with conversation about Dunkirk and how brave the men who owned the boats were to pick up England's soldiers, and what Hitler might do next.

Emily's eyes widened in bewilderment. Her modern attire dissolved into a soft floral dress typical of the 1940s, with a delicate hat perched atop her head. Her handbag felt lighter; she looked down, and it was now a small dark green bag with a brass clasp. To her left side was a cloth bag, dark green in colour, which held her gas mask. As she took her first hesitant step inside, an inexplicable sensation washed over her, and a gentle voice seemed to whisper in her ear, "Save your grandfather."

Her heartbeat quickened as she glanced around, her senses overwhelmed by the nostalgia and surreal familiarity of a bygone era. She felt as though she had plunged into a sepia-toned photograph, the world around her swirling with fragments of history she had read about in books or from the stories her grandfather had told her. She made her way to the bar, where the bartender, a stout man with rolled-up sleeves and a pipe dangling loosely from his lips, nodded his head toward her as though she were a regular.

"Ah, afternoon Miss Emily," he said, his voice rich with warmth and a hint of curiosity. "The usual, I suppose?"

Emily faltered for a moment, unsure how to respond, but words flowed from her as though they had been rehearsed many times before. "Yes, the usual please," she heard herself say, her voice carrying a cadence unfamiliar yet undeniably hers. He nodded, poured a measure of what looked like port or sherry into a small glass, and handed it to her. Emily took out her purse, but the bartender refused her money, saying, "The first one is on me," as he smiled and carried on wiping the glasses. Emily picked up her drink and looked for a seat in the bustling pub.

She noticed some men playing cards at a corner table, their laughter and shouts punctuating the air. Nearby, two women chatted quietly, heads close together as they shared secrets. She chose a cosy table near the fire, which crackled with warmth, and smiled at a woman sitting alone at a nearby table. The woman wore a thoughtful expression.

As Emily settled in, she took a moment to appreciate the warmth of the fire. She began to contemplate why she had been sent back in time to save her grandfather, how she was supposed to accomplish this task, whose voice was instructing her to do so, and how the bartender knew her name. Many questions filled her mind.

At that moment, a tall soldier with noticeable ginger hair entered the pub, drawing attention. A man announced, "Here he is, the man of the moment." The soldier, dressed in a slightly worn but polished uniform, proceeded to the bar. Several men gathered around him, eager to shake his hand and offer their congratulations or perhaps express their admiration.

Emily watched as the men gathered around the soldier, patting him on the back and waiting to hear his story. Suddenly, the woman who had been sitting at the nearby table stood up and moved over to Emily.

"Excuse me, my dear, do you mind if I join you?" The woman smiled at Emily as she placed her glass on the table and looked at Emily, waiting for an answer.

Emily smiled back and pulled out a chair for her. "Oh, please take a seat."

The woman placed her handbag under the table and adjusted herself. She picked up her drink, took a sip, then looked at Emily. "This might seem unusual to you, but please listen to me."

Emily looked at the woman with a puzzled expression. "It can't be any stranger than how my day is going," she replied.

The woman leaned closer to Emily and, in a whisper, said, "My name is Iaeculi. The reason you are here is to prevent your grandfather from being hit by the tram. There was a grievous error, and your grandfather should never have been harmed."

Before Iaeculi could continue, Emily interrupted. "Why is it my responsibility to rectify this situation? I did nothing wrong," Emily retorted sharply. "It is your mistake; you should fix it," she added, rising from her seat.

Iaeculi grasped Emily's wrist and pleaded, "Please allow me to explain. It is important that you do."

"Five minutes, no more, and then I am leaving," Emily responded, sitting back down.

"Thank you," Iaeculi replied, taking another sip of her drink before glancing over at the bar. "Do you see that soldier? That is your grandfather. In two days' time, he will be in a wheelchair. We, the watchers of time, cannot correct every error. We have made numerous mistakes, and as watchers, we are unable to intervene directly in the past. This is where you come in, my dear. People vanish, never to be seen again, because we asked them to assist us in repairing the timeline, and they chose not to return to their own time. You are invited here for a purpose, but if you do not return within four days, you will become lost in time."

All I am requesting is that you help your grandfather. By doing so, you will ensure the survival of others during the war. If he avoids that accident, he will go on to save a group of soldiers who were pinned down, and they, in turn, will save others. This is why you must save your grandfather. You save him, and in return, he saves others who go on to help others."

Iaeculi gazed at Emily, hoping she would choose to do the right thing. She continued, "Your grandfather, Terry, was a renowned strategist in his time. His knowledge and leadership were instrumental in several key battles during Dunkirk. If he is incapacitated, those soldiers will be left without his guidance. It's not just about saving him; it's about preserving the lives of many who depend on his expertise."

Emily's mind raced as she processed the information. She remembered stories her grandfather had told her and how upset he used to get about not being able to fight for his country because of the wheelchair. "How am I supposed to stop it?" Emily asked, her voice softer now, tinged with a mix of fear and determination.

Iaeculi regarded Emily with a smile. "He once posed the same question to your mother. The task was the same as yours—to stop the accident—but she deemed it too challenging and declined. I believe you are our last hope, and I believe you can succeed."

Emily stared thoughtfully into the fire, observing the flames as they sent sparks up the chimney and listening to each crackle. She seemed to be seeking answers, hopeful that the fire might offer some insight.

"Why did my mother never tell me about being asked to help?" Emily inquired, slowly turning her head towards Iaeculi.

"When you have completed what we ask, or in your mother's case, didn't do, you will be sent back, and you will completely forget all about us and the task we had assigned to you. We cannot have everyone knowing about us and time travel," replied Iaeculi, finishing her drink. The flickering flames from the fire cast a warm glow on her stern face, enhancing the air of mystery that surrounded her.

Emily fidgeted in her seat, her mind racing with the overwhelming responsibility thrust upon her. "So, how do I prevent the accident? I can't just approach him and say, 'Hi granddad, you don't know me yet, I am your future granddaughter Emily, and I'm here to inform you about an accident you're going to have.' I don't think he will buy it somehow, do you?" Emily said. Her voice wavered slightly as she spoke, revealing her anxiety.

She then picked up her glass and took a hesitant sip, grimacing as the unfamiliar taste hit her tongue. "What is this stuff? It's warm and tastes unpleasant," she remarked, putting her glass back on the table with a slight shudder.

"That's port. Women of this era didn't order pints of lager or ale; they drank milk stout, sherry, port, gin, and other drinks," Iaeculi said, trying not to laugh at Emily's expression as she tried to drink her port. Iaeculi continued, *"Go to your grandfather and tell him how proud you are of him and the other soldiers who made it back. Your words will resonate deeply with him, knowing that his bravery is recognised. Mention you are a friend of Doris, his wife, and praise the poem he wrote in one of his letters. Please recite the poem titled 'Before the Trumpets Call.' You've read it many times, so I believe you are familiar with it by heart now."*

My letter waits upon the windowsill,
My words restrained, yet trembling still.
I've kissed your lips a thousand times,

But none could hold me past the lines.

The war is far, but closer yet,

Than any oath we ever set.

It tugs at me with duty's weight,

And bids me walk through sorrow's gate.

I see your tears you try to hide,

As if your heart is untied.

But I am yours, in fire or frost,

No bullet makes that promise lost.

Remember me in morning light,

In birdsong soft, in stars at night.

Each beat of mine will echo true,

In every thought, I march to you.

But if I fall where poppies grow,

Let time be kind and gently show,

That love like ours will never part,

For even death can't steal the heart.

Iaeculi's Visit

"I miss him dearly," she said, her voice trembling. "I worry about him every single day. I pray every night for his safe return."

With a sigh, Iaeculi paused, her fingers brushing the edge of her handbag. She looked out of the window at the early morning light. "When you go to the butcher's," she continued, "accept that this is your last week at home before you return to your regiment."

She paused for a moment, then added, "I want to take you away for a few days – with me, our daughter, and my parents. I know it's not what you'd planned, but once you leave, I don't know when I'll see you again. That's why I'm planning this week away."

Her voice softened, but there was an unmistakable plea in it. "Don't be upset about not being able to spend a few days drinking with your mates. I've never asked for much, but now, this is all I'm asking."

Iaeculi picked up her handbag and stood up to leave. "Are you leaving already?" Emily asked, her voice filled with anxiety. "What if I need your assistance, or if he decides to leave?"

"You'll be fine," Iaeculi reassured her with a smile. "There are trigger words you can use to ensure he listens. Don't worry."

With that, Iaeculi walked towards the door, leaving Emily to wait. Emily observed the soldier, trying to steady her breath. She could hardly believe she was looking at her grandfather, young and full of life. It had been so long.

Emily's Conversation with Terry

After about five minutes, most of the other men returned to their seats. Emily saw her chance and, with a deep breath, approached the bar, her heart pounding in her chest. She stood in front of the man she knew so well — yet so differently now.

"Good afternoon, sir," she said, trying to steady her voice. The urge to embrace him, to hold him once more, was overwhelming. Her heart raced as she took in the familiar lines of his face, now younger and full of life.

Terry took a step back, startled by her presence. "Good afternoon, Miss. May I ask who you are?" he replied, smiling warmly. He placed his pint on the counter and extended his hand.

Emily hesitated before shaking his hand. The hum of chatter in the pub contrasted with the whirlwind of thoughts in her mind. "My name is Emily Lroft. I'm a friend of Doris, your wife. She's spoken so highly of you. I was wondering if you have a few minutes to spare?"

Terry smiled. "It's nice to meet you, Emily. Of course, I have plenty of time to chat. Would you prefer to stand here, or would you like to sit somewhere?" He gestured towards a small table by the window, where the sunlight streamed in, casting warm patterns on the floor.

Emily nodded, and they made their way over to the table. Each step felt surreal to her as she walked beside the man she had only known in a wheelchair. Once seated, Terry pulled out a chair for Emily with a gentlemanly gesture before sitting across from her.

"So, what would you like to discuss?" Terry asked, his voice tinged with curiosity. "Please tell me Doris isn't messing about with someone else, as I'm not sure I could handle that," he added, taking a contemplative sip of his beer. His eyes searched Emily's face for reassurance.

Emily's expression remained calm but serious. "No, Doris isn't messing with anyone else," she began, offering him a small smile of reassurance. "I just want to let you know what Doris has been experiencing while you've been away," she added, pausing to collect her thoughts.

She was trying to recall everything Iaeculi had told her. Emily then looked at Terry and explained everything, even managing to recite the poem without missing any of the verses.

Terry finished the last of his beer, glanced at the empty glass, and turned to Emily. "When I was in France, evading bullets and German patrols while making my way to Dunkirk, the thought of seeing Doris and my daughter again was the only thing that kept me going," he said, his voice heavy with memory. "However, upon returning home and knowing Doris was safe, all I wanted was to spend time with my mates before rejoining my regiment. Emily, you've given me a much-needed kick up the arse. I was planning to stay here until some of my pals arrived, but now, I'm going home to spend the evening with Doris, whether it's at home or in some air raid shelter. Rest assured, I won't mention the week away — your secret is safe with me."

With that, Terry stood up and gave Emily a brief peck on the cheek. A mix of gratitude and determination filled him as he walked through the dimly lit pub, his heavy boots echoing against the floorboards. Emily watched him leave, a smile tugging at the corners of her lips. She appreciated the bond they shared and the stories he had told her while she was growing up. She would have loved to tell him who she really was, but if she did, what would have happened? She was proud to have spent some time with him again.

As he reached the door, Terry put on his side cap and glanced back at Emily one last time. He smiled before stepping out into the brisk air, ready to embrace the warmth and love waiting for him at home.

Her emotions intensified, and tears welled up. However, she managed to bid farewell to her grandfather one final time. Composing herself, she took one last glance around the pub. Upon stepping out, she found herself back in her own time, no longer in the 1940s. The modern world felt stark and jarring after the quiet nostalgia of the past.

Then, she stopped dead in the street. She had a déjà vu moment, as if she had been here before. It took her a moment, but then she remembered: she was outside the Pipe Makers Arms. Due to Emily's efforts in saving her grandfather from his accident, he was able to save many lives thereafter. As a result, the Second World War ended in 1948, as is well remembered.

Many individuals experience moments when they feel an uncanny sense of familiarity with their surroundings or premonitions about upcoming events. This phenomenon, often referred to as déjà vu, raises questions about whether it is merely a psychological occurrence or if there may be external influences prompting us to assist in some capacity. We will never know. There may be events that have changed without our awareness. Saving one person's life can lead to numerous changes. Every individual is valuable and worthy of saving. If you were not here, how many lives would be affected?

Chapter 2
Faces of Gullveig

Ron Talbot greatly enjoys spending weekends with his wife, Donna. Together, they go out searching for historical artefacts with their metal detectors. Over the years, they have discovered numerous coins, a Norman sword, a Roman bracelet, and, of course, plenty of modern rubbish. They often spend their evenings researching the origins of their finds and documenting them in a detailed journal. Their shared passion has led them to connect with a community of fellow enthusiasts, exchanging tips and stories about their discoveries.

One day, they decided to travel to France for a week in their camper van to explore several fields. With permission from the landowner, they began their search.

During the first few days, they found remnants from the First World War and some items from the Second World War. The couple marvelled at the history these objects represented, imagining the lives of those who once owned them.

On the third morning, midway through their search, Ron discovered a solid gold ring adorned with intricate markings along the band. He decided to rinse it with the water from his bottle, and it seemed to glow and whisper his name. The ring's unique craftsmanship captivated him, as it appeared to be ancient and potentially linked to a significant historical event.

Ron examined the exquisite engravings that adorned the band, noticing symbols that suggested a connection to an old legend he had once read about. Without much thought, Ron tried the ring on, and it fit perfectly. The sensation of the cold, wet metal against his skin gave him a strange sense of belonging. However, when he tried to remove it, the ring would not budge. It merely twisted around his finger, its grip feeling almost alive. He stood up and called out to Donna for assistance, but she also could not remove the ring, despite her best efforts. She even tried using some hand cream from her rucksack, but it was in vain.

As they struggled, the ring seemed to tighten with each attempt, and a voice resonated in Ron's mind, saying, "Change your face, change your fate." The words echoed deeply within him, sending chills down his spine and leaving him in bewilderment and concern.

Donna suggested they return to the camper van to assess the situation with a clearer mind. As they walked back, the weight of the ring seemed to grow heavier on Ron's finger, almost as if it were urging him to act. Despite his unease, he couldn't ignore the ring's pull—fascinating and terrifying at once.

Later that evening, seated at the small foldable table inside the camper, Ron and Donna examined the ring under a magnifying glass. They noted the engravings in greater detail, realising that the symbols resembled ancient runes—possibly connected to Nordic mythology. Donna scribbled notes in their journal as Ron described the symbols to her.

Their research led them to an obscure legend about a ring crafted by a master artisan for a Viking warrior. The ring was said to embody the spirit of transformation and destiny, capable of revealing truths hidden within those who wore it. As they delved deeper into the story, a chilling detail emerged—the ring was also believed to bind itself to those unworthy, consuming their identity until they became shadows of their former selves.

Ron and Donna exchanged nervous glances. All their years of exploring history had never led them to something so eerie, so alive. They decided it was time to contact an expert—someone who could decipher the ring's markings and perhaps unravel its mysteries. But as Ron pulled out his mobile phone, the whispers in his mind turned into an unmistakable command: "For the sake of your life, you must not let it go." His hand trembled, and then the phone seemed to be pulled from his grip, flying across the camper.

Donna looked up from her journal and glanced over at Ron. "Are you okay?" she asked, removing her glasses and placing them on the journal.

Ron appeared unsettled, glancing at his hand and then at the phone. "I don't know. I can hear a voice in my head."

Donna walked over to Ron and knelt down in front of him. She placed her hands around his hand and asked, "What is the voice saying?"

Ron looked at Donna with apprehension. "It's just one voice, and it's telling me something about changing my face, changing my fate, and not to take the ring off because it will endanger my life.”

“Ron, this ring is more than just jewellery,” Donna stated, her eyes narrowing as she leaned closer. “It possesses some kind of ancient power or spell. What if the voice you hear is somehow connected to the ring?”

Ron’s eyes widened in disbelief. “But I don’t understand. What if the ring affects me negatively?” His hands trembled as he examined the ring, turning it in different directions, its intricate patterns gleaming under the light.

Donna looked around thoughtfully, her mind racing. “If the ring was made by the master artisan for some Viking warrior, how did he lose it? And how come it was found just a few inches deep? And who owned it after this Viking?”

The camper van fell silent, the air thick with tension. Suddenly, Ron grew very pale and began shaking uncontrollably as a cold, eerie voice echoed in his mind: “I am Gullveig, and I was a handmaiden to Freya. You cannot escape your destiny. Make your choices wisely.”

Ron’s lips quivered as he repeated the words to Donna, his voice barely a whisper.

Donna spoke firmly, her tone resolute. “Ron, you need to remove that ring. Whatever the voice is warning you about, it’s not good.”

But Ron hesitated, holding the ring tightly as if his life depended on it. “What if I lose everything? What if the voice is right?” He looked at

Donna with fear in his eyes, searching for reassurance.

Donna placed a comforting hand on his shoulder. "We'll figure this out together. You are not alone. But we must be cautious." Her eyes shone with determination, masking the uncertainty she felt deep inside.

They decided to shorten their break and return home to figure out how to remove the ring without endangering Ron's life. Donna started to put her journal away in her rucksack and tidy up the fold-up table. Ron glanced at a magazine cover lying on the dashboard. It featured an actor recently involved in a scandal, displaying expressions of regret and defiance. The bold headlines and glossy finish made the actor's features stand out dramatically. As Ron looked at the image, he experienced an unusual sensation—a tingling on his face, then a strange warmth spreading across it. Within minutes, his features began shifting subtly but noticeably, until he resembled the actor completely, including the small scar under the right eye. His hair colour changed to match the actor's exact shade, and even his eyes altered their hue.

Confused and disoriented, Ron touched his face, feeling the unfamiliar contours—the broader jawline, the higher cheekbones, and the distinct dimple on his chin. He turned his gaze towards the camper van's interior mirror. The reflection staring back at him was unmistakably the actor's face. Panic set in as he realised his entire appearance had morphed. Ron rubbed his hands over his face repeatedly, hoping the transformation would reverse, but it remained unchanged.

Donna turned to Ron, her jaw dropping as her eyes locked onto the unfamiliar face before her. "Ron, what is happening to you?" she stammered, her voice tinged with fear. She instinctively grabbed her mobile phone, hoping to find some kind of answer on the internet.

"I don't know!" Ron exclaimed, his voice now emanating in a deep American accent. "The ring—it must be the ring that has caused this!" He struggled with the jewel, but the more he attempted to remove it, the tighter it seemed to adhere to his finger, as though it possessed life, pulsing with a faint warmth.

Donna paused her search on a website about Norse mythology. "Gullveig was reputed to be a master of magic and illusions. She was a handmaiden, stabbed with spears, but she couldn't die. They threw her into a fire, but she came out unscathed. Then they threw her into the fire again, and still, she emerged untouched. This is when she took the name Heidr, meaning 'the gleaming one' in Norse. 'Gull' in Norse means gold, and 'Veig' means intoxication or strength," she murmured. "If she truly is connected to this ring, then perhaps this transformation is part of her manipulations. But why would she desire this?"

Ron groaned, clutching his head before collapsing to his knees. Gullveig's voice grew louder and more insistent: "This is your first, but not your last. You fool, you desired to don the ring, and now you shall perceive the world through many eyes. Your path lies ahead, but the choices are yours to make. Will you embrace this power, or be crushed by it?"

Donna swiftly moved to Ron's side, shaking him gently in an

effort to bring him back to reality. "Ron, listen to me. Whatever this is—it's trying to control you. But we won't let it. You can discover a way to break this curse. You need to fight it with everything you have got."

Ron's breathing became shallow, his hands trembling as he grasped the ring. "I can't... I can't hold on, it feels as if I am being drained," he whispered. His new appearance, eerily calm yet unnervingly foreign, looked up at Donna.

Donna resumed her search online, looking for scholars, mythologists, and even paranormal investigators who might provide insights into removing the ring. Her fingers trembled as she navigated through the pages. "We will find a solution, Ron," Donna affirmed, her voice steady despite the fear lurking beneath. "But first, I need you to trust me. Whatever this ring makes you do, it cannot take away who you are. Try and see if you can get your face back."

Ron nodded, feeling lost yet anchored by Donna's resolve. He leaned against the camper van for a while, then slowly got to his feet. He steadied himself and then made his way into the camper van, the small space now feeling like sanctuary. He sat down heavily and started to think about his own face—the face he did not want to lose. Much though was tangled with the dread of losing his face completely.

As he sat there concentrating with great effort, he closed his eyes and reflected on his face—the face he wanted back, noting the grey strands in his goatee and the wrinkles that once surrounded his eyes. Then he felt a warmth beginning to spread across his head, followed by a tingling sensation that escalated into a burning pain, as though his face were on fire. He instinctively brought his hands to his face. Although the discomfort lasted only a few minutes, it seemed much longer.

Ron paused briefly to focus his vision, then stood up and glanced into the exterior mirror. His original face had returned, and the American actor's face had disappeared. He called out to Donna and realised his voice had also reverted. Donna appeared at the doorway of the camper van, her expression shocked.

"How did you regain your face? Did you manage to remove that cursed ring?" she asked, looking down at his hand. "Come on, let's pack up and return home before anything else happens," she added.

Ron smiled at Donna. "I had to think about my face, and then after a burning pain, it appeared. The pain was so bad, I wanted to cry out, but no sound came out. I think I know how to handle the ring now."

Ron exited the van with a smile, thoughts racing through his mind about who he could become next. He considered the minor discomfort worthwhile for the opportunity to transform into someone else. He folded the chairs and placed them in the camper van. Roughly ten minutes later, they were heading home.

As days passed, Ron's transformations became uncontrollable. He could shift his face at will, and with Gullveig helping him learn how to use the ring, he found it less painful. Ron experimented, transforming into various people—friends, strangers, historical figures he admired. Each change felt exhilarating, empowering. But with each change, he felt more emotionally distant from his original self, a strange fatigue creeping in. He began losing his sense of identity.

Donna, frightened yet fascinated, warned him, "This isn't normal. You need to find out how to remove the ring."

Ron had grown accustomed to the ring and became comfortable with it, feeling that removing it would be like losing a companion. He was beginning to understand its power, but he knew it drained him each time he used it. The ring glowed faintly, casting a soft shimmer over his hand— a constant reminder of the weight it carried.

One afternoon, while sitting in the garden and doing his crossword puzzle, surrounded by vibrant flowers and the gentle rustling of leaves, Gullveig spoke to him. "Be cautious. You have used the ring frequently and not wisely. The consequences of your actions are for you to decide." Ron placed the paper on his lap and looked into the garden, pondering what Gullveig's words meant. The sunlight filtered through the treetops, creating dappled patterns on the ground, and he felt a chill despite the warmth of the day. Could this be a warning of impending danger or a sign that he needed to change his ways? The serene environment contrasted sharply with the turmoil brewing within him as he wrestled with the implications of Gullveig's prophetic advice.

Ron sighed deeply, the air around him growing heavier with each passing thought. He clutched the ring instinctively, feeling its reassuring warmth against his skin, even as Gullveig's warning echoed in his ears. A sparrow darted past him, its wings catching the sunlight, and for a brief moment, he envied its freedom. His hand trembled slightly as he picked up the paper again, but the words blurred before him, their meanings slipping away like sand through his fingers.

"We must be cautious," he murmured under his breath, though a part of him rebelled against the notion. The ring had become a part of him, a second heartbeat, a whisper in the dark corners of his mind. Yet, he could not deny the growing unease, the sense that each decision made with the ring pulled him closer to a precipice he could neither see nor fully comprehend.

As the minutes ticked by, the garden seemed to transform around him. The once-gentle rustling of the leaves grew into an ominous murmur, as though the trees were whispering secrets to one another—secrets they dared not share with him. The sunlight, too, began to shift, its golden hues deepening into amber, casting long shadows that seemed to crawl toward him with every passing breath.

Ron stood abruptly, the ring now feeling heavier, almost alive in his grasp. It pulsed faintly, an almost imperceptible rhythm that matched the thudding of his heart. He turned toward the house, its familiar outlines now appearing distant and blurred, as if shrouded by unseen haze.

A sudden gust of wind swept through the garden, scattering petals into the air like a fleeting storm of colour. Hidden within the wind's howl, he thought he heard a voice. It was faint, almost indistinguishable from the rustling leaves, yet unmistakable in its intent.

"Decide now, Ron, before we decide for you."

He shivered and took an unsteady step forward, his feet crunching against the gravel path. The weight of choice hung heavily over him, and for the first time, he felt the true cost of the power he had come to rely on. Could he somehow remove the ring and walk away from its power and strength? Or was he bound to it, as inseparably as the light is to day?

"I will need more time," he murmured with a strained voice.

In response, the garden's restless energy subsided, resulting in a profound silence. The ring began to emit a radiant glow, accompanied by a warmth that spread through Ron's body. He collapsed to the ground, feeling dizzy as the ring pulled him into its essence. He was merging with the ring, while the garden's colours blended seamlessly around him.

Ron opened his eyes slowly. He found himself standing in an unfamiliar landscape, one that seemed to exist both within and outside of himself. The ground beneath his feet shimmered with iridescent hues, constantly shifting and pulsing as if breathing with life. Above him, the sky was an endless expanse of swirling light, a tapestry of colours that defied comprehension. He felt weightless, as though he floated on the cusp of existence, yet the ring's presence anchored him, its pulse now harmonising with the rhythm of this strange domain.

Ron experienced a mix of fear and excitement. His hand felt unusual, tingling as he looked down at it and noticed that the ring had vanished. His heart pounded as he tried to figure out where he was, surveying his surroundings.

A figure suddenly emerged from the kaleidoscopic landscape, her form flickering and constantly shifting as if woven from the very fabric of this strange world. She wore a long white dress adorned with gold trim around the collar and cuffs, and her skin glowed with an ethereal light that seemed to emanate from within. As she moved, the hem of her dress fluttered gracefully, making her appear almost weightless, as though she were gliding over the ground rather than walking.

Her voice was warm and soothing, speaking slowly and clearly. The words seemed to resonate deeply within him, echoing through his mind and soul. Every syllable she uttered felt like a gentle caress, calming his fears and filling him with a sense of peace. The air around her shimmered with a faint golden hue, adding to the surreal quality of her presence. Ron felt an inexplicable connection to her, as if she held the answers to questions he hadn't even asked yet.

"Ron," she said, smiling. "My name is Gullveig, and you have crossed into the domain of the ring's essence. You had your chance to use the ring wisely and chose not to. Now, we have decided that the ring must have been too powerful for you. We were aware that you loved the ring, and with this in mind, we decided to make you part of the ring."

Ron felt as though the ground beneath him dissolved into nothingness, leaving him suspended in the weightless expanse of this enigmatic new world. Her words echoed in his ears, weaving threads of confusion and clarity into an intricate tapestry of understanding. He opened his mouth to speak but found himself voiceless; the only sound was the gentle hum of the world around him, as though it were alive, breathing with him.

Gullveig stepped closer, her presence like the warmth and glow of sunlight filtering through darkness. She raised her hand, and with a graceful motion, conjured a vision before him. The shimmering lights coalesced into a mirror-like surface, revealing his reflection. But the image did not show the Ron he remembered—it depicted a being of pure radiance, his outline subtly intertwined with the ring's essence. His form pulsated with a quiet power, his features more ethereal than human.

"This is who you are, Ron," she continued, her voice both tender and resolute. "You have transcended the boundaries of the material world, becoming one with the energy that the ring embodies. The decisions you once struggled with are no longer yours to make; they are fragments of a larger purpose. Accept this truth, and you will find peace within the chaos."

His mind raced as he grappled with her words. Every fibre of his being felt both liberated and bound, caught in a paradox of freedom and servitude. Yet, through the storm of thoughts, he felt a growing clarity—a realisation that perhaps this was not the end of himself, but the beginning of something greater than he had ever imagined.

Gullveig walked toward Ron and extended her hand, a gesture of invitation. "Come, Ron. There is much for you to learn, and even more for you to become. The essence of the ring touches everything, every living thread in this world. You are now part of that infinite weave. Trust in what you are becoming and walk forward."

Ron hesitated, staring at her hand as if it held the key to a door he could not see. With a breath that felt like the last act of his former self, he reached out, his fingers brushing against hers. As their connection forged, the world around them erupted into a symphony of light and sound—an overwhelming cascade of sensations that pulled him deeper into his transformation.

And then, just as suddenly as it had begun, the storm subsided. Ron found himself in a new expanse of the realm—a place where colours danced gently in harmony, and the air hummed with serene energy. He no longer felt out of place; he felt whole. Somewhere deep within, he understood that this was not the end, nor was it his beginning. It was simply his becoming.

In life, we sometimes come across valuable opportunities, whether they appear as information, friendship, or unexpected discoveries. It is our responsibility to use these opportunities wisely and avoid misuse. Some things are beyond our understanding, and abusing such opportunities can lead to serious consequences. For example, Ron found a ring but failed to use it wisely, which did not end too well for him. Ultimately, how we handle these opportunities shapes our destiny and influences those around us. By practising mindfulness, empathy, and ethical judgement, we contribute positively to our community and the world at large.

Chapter 3
The Station Master

Just outside Eldersham village stands Bullgreen station, abandoned and left to rot—a ghostly reminder of times past. The paint peels, revealing layers of history hidden beneath its worn exterior, and its sign creaks ominously in the wind, sounding like whispers from bygone days. Originally opened on July 6th, 1903, it served as a bustling hub for travellers and traders. Designed in the Victorian architectural style, it featured intricate brickwork and arched windows. In its heyday, Bullgreen station was vital to the community, connecting Eldersham to larger cities and fostering economic growth. However, by 1964, it was abandoned due to Dr Beeching's restructuring of the British railway system, which aimed to cut costs by closing less profitable lines. The once-thriving station now stands as a relic of the past, a silent witness to the village's rich history and the changing tides of transportation.

The platforms that once welcomed passengers are now empty and overgrown with wild grasses and weeds, giving them an eerie, forgotten appearance. Ivy clings to the walls, creating a tangled green blanket that slowly consumes the building, while most of the windows are broken, their shattered glass glinting in the sunlight like sad remnants of its former glory. Moss has started to creep along the edges of the roof and surrounding area. It is silent, except for the occasional rustle of leaves and the distant sound of birdsong. Bullgreen station stands as a poignant relic of Eldersham's history, evoking nostalgia and curiosity about the stories it once held.

The door to the ticket office, dilapidated and hanging on one hinge, is surrounded by cobwebs that capture insects and small leaves. The rusted metal handle barely clings to the rotten wood. Upon entering, there is an opening where tickets were once purchased, its edges worn from years of use. Dust particles dance in the soft light filtering through the broken windows. To the right, a doorway leads into the office, where faded posters for long-gone train routes cling stubbornly to chipped walls. This office, once clean and tidy—the heart of the station—now lies ransacked, its windows smashed. An old wooden desk sits in the corner, littered with outdated timetables and yellowed receipts. The wooden floor, now covered in dust, old beer cans, and fallen plaster from the ceiling, still carries the scent of aged wood, mingling with the musty aroma of mildew. Broken boards creak underfoot, and a damp chill permeates the air, hinting at leaks in the roof, the ceiling marred by time and water damage.

Small creatures scurry across the floor, finding shelter among the debris, while the eeriness of the abandoned office envelops any visitor brave enough to enter. At the back of the office is another doorway leading into a workshop room, cluttered with disused equipment and tarnished train parts. The air is thick with the scent of rust and neglect, a silent testament to the station's dormant days. Fragments of shattered glass sparkle faintly in the dim light, scattered amidst piles of old rags and discarded tools. Above, a single, exposed bulb dangles from a frayed wire, swaying gently in the breeze that comes through the broken windows.

Along the platform stands the waiting room, its door long gone, and the wooden benches now absent. The cream-coloured walls that once advertised holiday destinations are now marred with graffiti—some depicting vivid yet haunting scenes, while others are mere scribbles left by passing vandals. The wooden roof beams, once sturdy, now sag with cobwebs, resembling old net curtains. Some beams house birds' nests, while a few roof tiles are broken, allowing the weather to seep in. Raindrops occasionally drip through the gaps, creating small puddles on the floor, which have stained the wood over time. The wooden floor is now scattered with leaves and twigs mixed with coal that once fed the fire during the colder months. On one wall stands the old fireplace, now filled with debris and forgotten memories.

Nature has begun reclaiming the area, with small plants sprouting between the floorboards, and insects making their homes in the crevices. The air hangs heavy with the smell of damp wood and decay, a stark contrast to the bustling activity the room once witnessed in its prime.

In the corner stands the ghostly figure of Mr. Tinker, the station master. He is dressed in his uniform, presenting a pristine appearance, ever vigilant, as though anticipating an arrival or event. Appointed as station master in 1921, he managed the station with great pride. However, in 1936, after completing his morning report and rising from his chair to make a cup of tea, he suffered a heart attack and collapsed, clutching his chest. Jim Dooley, the porter, discovered him twenty minutes later, slumped on the floor. From that day onward, tales of Mr. Tinker's ghostly presence began circulating among the station staff and passengers. Some claimed to feel a chill as they passed the ticket counter, while others swore they saw a fleeting shadow in the corner of their eye. Despite these eerie encounters, the station continued to function, with Jim Dooley stepping up to fill the role of station master, always respectful of his predecessor's memory. The legend of Mr. Tinker became an integral part of the station's history, a reminder of the dedication and service that defined its past.

Mr. Tinker was unable to move on. He was happy at Bullgreen station, enjoying chatting with passengers, and not being married meant he could dedicate more time to the job he loved. After the station closed in 1964, he felt frustrated, considering the station to be of greater significance to the people of Eldersham than the government's cost-saving measures. Mr. Tinker frequently roamed the station, watching visitors explore the abandoned building. Some individuals would vandalise the place—breaking windows or pulling down drainpipes. Others came to take photographs, while a few would try to burn the station down by lighting small fires. But Mr. Tinker would always put them out. Others used his former office for private encounters, which annoyed him. He would try to scare them off, but it never seemed to work.

One day, a young man, about eighteen years old, entered the station, causing disruption by kicking objects and spraying paint on the walls. The room was dimly lit, filled with old rags, tools, and bottles of oil. He took out a small penknife from his pocket and began carving his name onto the workbench, which bore the marks of previous carvings. Observing this, Mr. Tinker approached the young man and inquired:

"What do you think you're doing to my workbench, sonny?" Mr. Tinker's voice was firm, with an undertone of displeasure, his hope that the young man could clearly hear him and stop what he was doing.

Startled, the young man looked around. Mr. Tinker stood with his hands on his hips, his face unnervingly pale. His eyes seemed to pierce through the young man's soul. The young man stumbled against the workbench, then tried to run, but it felt as though invisible hands were holding him in place. He attempted to call out, but no sound emerged.

The young man stood there, visibly anxious, as the room seemed to grow colder, his heart racing wildly.

"Please remain calm and explain why you feel the need to damage my station," Mr. Tinker requested, stepping closer with an eerie calmness that made the room feel even colder.

"Who the hell are you? I came here because this place is usually deserted, and I needed somewhere to think. Since it's no longer owned by anyone, I thought I could mark the walls with my tag and carve my name on the bench," the young man replied, scanning the workshop for an escape route.

"So, you are alone?" Mr. Tinker asked, glancing around the workshop. "It appears you believe you can come here and act as you wish. This is my station, and I would appreciate it if people respected my home." His voice rose slightly. "Do I make myself clear?"

"But I thought this place was abandoned, and no one lived here. I didn't mean any harm. I'm truly sorry," the young man said, cautiously moving towards the door. "How long have you lived here, mate? And why haven't you done the place up a bit?"

"I have lived here since 1921, and I would like to restore the station to its previous condition, but that is not within my capability," Mr. Tinker replied, moving closer to the door and watching the young man's every action carefully.

"The year is 201… How on earth have you been here since 1921? What are you, a ghost or something?" The young man asked, looking surprised and a bit spooked. He attempted to run towards the door, but Mr. Tinker gestured with his hand, and the door slammed shut, sending dust everywhere. The young man froze, looking for another exit, but the only other way out was behind Mr. Tinker.

"Yes, I am a spirit, a restless one at that," Mr. Tinker said. "I can also read people. I know things about you, David Marchant. I feel your guilt. There's something you want to change in your past. I can help with that. If you could change one thing, what would it be? Choose wisely. Some changes might negatively affect your future." He looked at David, waiting for an answer.

"How do you know my name, and what information do you have about me?" David inquired, his expression strained as he pointed at Mr. Tinker. He paused, scrutinising the ghostly figure before him, then turned toward the workbench and gazed out of the broken window, watching the trees sway in the breeze. His thoughts were occupied with reflections on his past, wondering how anyone could possibly know his previous actions. After a moment, he leaned back against the workbench and redirected his attention to Mr. Tinker.

"How is it possible that you can read me so accurately? We just met, yet you seem to know everything about me—my deceit, my wrongdoings. Is it truly possible to know all this merely by observing someone? During your lifetime, did you work in a circus, or did you hold a more important position?" David asked, folding his arms, his mind racing as he tried to comprehend how this stranger could possess such knowledge about him.

Mr. Tinker regarded David with a calm, almost serene expression, a faint smile playing at the corner of his lips. "I was the station master," he began, his voice steady. "This station, once a beautiful place, was both my work and my life. I passed away in the other room and have remained here ever since. What I do is not merely observation or some circus trick. I can see deep into people's souls and read them like a book. I have mastered this over the years. Since working with trains is no longer an option for me, I have decided to work with people. I send them on a journey into their past to rectify a mistake. However, if they make the wrong choice, it becomes a one-way journey."

Mr. Tinker's eyes followed David's every move, his gaze sharp and knowing. He could feel the weight of David's regrets, the things that haunted him daily. "You see," he continued, "I know you have deep regrets. I know they play on your mind constantly."

"I should be running scared right now, but... but there's something interesting in what you say," David admitted, his voice shaky but curious. "Sorry, what is your name? Or should I just call you the station master?"

"You can call me Mr. Tinker, or station master, whichever you prefer," Mr. Tinker replied. "You likely have many questions, but know this: if you want to correct your past, it must be done sincerely, not out of greed. If I determine that it's the wrong choice, I'll send you back without revealing whether it was the right one. If it was the wrong choice, I'll send you back before you were born and give someone else your life. You'll return before the mistake occurred, and you'll have two days to fix it—no more. You can't tell anyone about this or about me. If you do, I'll end your life and give someone else the chance to live in your place. All you have to do is think about the time and the place, and you will arrive there. If you come back, you won't remember anything. These are my rules. Do you understand?"

Mr. Tinker's voice was calm yet commanding, echoing through the dimly lit room as he watched David carefully, waiting for him to grasp the full weight of his words.

David's eyes widened as he absorbed the gravity of the situation. "But what if I fail? What happens then?" he stammered, his heart pounding as a thousand thoughts raced through his mind.

Mr. Tinker's gaze softened slightly. "Failure is part of the journey of life. Some you win, and some you lose. But it doesn't mean you never tried. This chance is unique and rare, a gift to help you make things right. Think carefully about your actions." He pulled out his pocket watch from his waistcoat pocket, held it in his hand, and then said, "Time is precious and fleeting. Use it wisely."

David nodded slowly, the gravity of Mr. Tinker's words sinking in. He felt a mix of trepidation and resolve, aware of the weight of the opportunity before him. The world around him seemed to hum with a strange energy. He understood that this chance, this moment, was fragile and fleeting. With a deep breath, he steadied himself, his mind already racing with plans and thoughts about how he would make things right. David knew this was not just a second chance, but perhaps the only chance he would ever get to correct his past and forge a new path forward.

"I believe I know what changes I wish to make, but I am concerned about the potential consequences if I fail and find myself somewhere I don't know," David inquired, his expression betraying a hint of apprehension.

"People have varying beliefs about Heaven and Hell," Mr. Tinker remarked, his tone steady. "Some believe in life after death, while others consider death final, like turning the light off. Your destiny following your choice depends on your belief system, David. Ultimately, whatever decision you make from your heart will seem the right one to you."

Mr. Tinker turned and began walking towards the door of the workshop.

The room fell silent as David looked down at his trainers, contemplating his decision. He hoped that making the right choice would restore normality, revive his father, and bring happiness to his mother, who would no longer need to drown her sorrows in drink, and maybe keep her job. Although there were other options David had considered, this one seemed the most viable.

David's heartbeat echoed in his ears as he recalled the turbulent events of the past few years. His father's fall from the roof, the argument that had led to it, had thrown the family into disarray. His mother had turned to alcohol to cope with the stress and grief. The once lively house was now filled with eerie silence and the occasional sound of muffled sobbing.

The weight of responsibility rested heavily on David's shoulders, but he knew he had to act for the sake of his mother. He meticulously reviewed each option, weighing the potential consequences and benefits. It was a leap of faith, but it was one he was willing to take for the love of his mother.

"David, have you made your decision? I can give you more time if needed," Mr. Tinker asked, glancing down at his pocket watch. He then grasped the door handle and turned it slowly. "When I open this door, you will need to walk through, and hopefully, you will find yourself where you desire to be."

"I have considered this decision carefully, and I do not need any more time," David replied, standing upright and taking a deep breath. "I am ready, and I believe I have made the correct decision. After this, my life will return to normal." David looked toward the door and said, "Okay, let's do this," before walking over to it.

Mr. Tinker opened the door, allowing a cold, sharp breeze to blow out, followed by a thick white mist that filled the dimly lit room. The breeze made David shiver. "Please proceed through. You'll be fine, I assure you," Mr. Tinker said, holding the door wide open. His eyes gleamed with strange intensity, watching David's every move.

David looked at the door and the mist emanating from it, his heart pounding in his chest. He could see faint shapes shifting within the mist, almost as if it were alive.

"There's no time like the present," David remarked, trying to muster enough courage, before stepping through the door and disappearing into the mist.

Mr. Tinker slowly closed the door behind him and then said, "The soul now departing is the 16.45, calling at station Lucifer in the next few minutes. Bloody teenagers today will believe anything you tell them. Let that be a lesson, David: never damage someone's property, especially when they have a deal with Lucifer."

His voice echoed throughout the desolate workshop, creating a persistent sense of dread that lingered in the air like a dark cloud. The room returned to a chilling silence as Mr. Tinker advanced toward his office. His steps were silent on the wooden floor, and upon reaching his office door, he stopped, casting one last wary glance around the eerie workshop before slipping inside.

Some abandoned buildings seem devoid of life. However, lurking within the shadows, sinister entities may be watching and waiting, guarding their old haunts with malevolent intent. Their icy presence can creep over your skin, or you might catch fleeting, spectral figures from the corner of your eye. An unsettling feeling that you are being watched intensifies with every step. What begins as a thrilling exploration could quickly turn into a nightmare, cloaked in mystery and rife with dangers that test the limits of even the bravest souls. Trespassing in those forsaken structures carries grave risks—an unknown fate awaits those who dare to enter, as the vengeful spirits of the past may not let intruders leave unscathed.

Chapter 4
Lens of the Asylum

The approach to Barnhill Asylum was along a narrow road, flanked by crumbling stone walls. Weeds pressed against the tyres, the overgrown path marred by numerous potholes. The asylum itself loomed beyond rusted gates that had remained open since the departure of the last patient years ago. The route to the asylum was overgrown, marked by a hulking silhouette—its brown windows darkened by grime and the passage of time. Paint peeled from heavy wooden doors, tangled ivy crawled up the façade, obscuring faded signage. Damp air and creeping sea mist contributed to the oppressive atmosphere.

George Crouch parked his van at the main entrance of the asylum, turned off the engine, and watched as the mist drifted around his vehicle.

He leaned forward to study the derelict building before releasing his seatbelt. For a moment, he remained seated, hands on the steering wheel, perhaps contemplating his next move. Only the subdued beat of his heart and the faint sound of dry leaves skittering across the ground disturbed the silence.

The salty tang of the sea hung heavily in the air, mixing with the earthy scent of decaying undergrowth. George's breath fogged the window screen as he waited. Every detail seemed amplified in the eerie quiet—from the soft patter of water droplets on the roof of his van to the distant echo of herring gulls calling above the mist. Each sound heightened the sense of anticipation. Finally, he exited the van, bracing himself for the unknown.

He pulled out his phone and located the email he had received from the historical society:

Dear Mr. Crouch,

Thank you for accepting the job to photograph Barnhill Asylum. We require this job to be carried out as soon as possible, due to the building being earmarked for demolition soon. Could you please photograph all remaining rooms before demolition in three weeks? We require both interior and exterior photos, as well as any remaining outside buildings, if they still exist. Please deliver high-resolution images, and if you could get these to us within three weeks, that would be appreciated. If you encounter any problems, please contact the office.

Kind regards,

Sara Longfellow.

It was a decent payday for a few hours' work. Barnhill had been abandoned since 1995—shut down after a series of administrative failings—the polite, bureaucratic euphemism for whatever really happened there.

George opened the side door of his van, slinging his camera bag over his shoulder and carrying the tripod under his arm. The building loomed before him, its blocks of dark red brick, windows gaping black—

many shattered. The main doors hung askew, one nearly off its hinges. He noticed the faint tang of bleach even from his van, as though someone had tried to scrub away three decades of dirt and dust.

Inside, the entrance hall was silent. The floor tiles were cracked, uneven, and some were missing; others had fallen, revealing the skeletal remains of a ceiling. On the left were the former lift shafts, filled with rubbish and broken furniture. Nearby was a set of concrete stairs with green-painted iron handrails. Debris—plaster fragments, broken bottles, and food wrappers—was scattered on the stairs.

Dim light filtered through grimy windows, casting distorted shadows that made the reception area feel colder. The air was thick with dust and the faint smell of mould, mingling with the acrid scent of rust and stagnant water. Paint peeled in great sheets from the walls, revealing patches of discoloured plaster beneath.

Parts of the ceiling were covered in black mould, and most of the light fixtures were either missing or hanging down, swaying on their wires with the breeze. George stepped forward, the ground crunching underfoot as if protesting the rare intrusion. The noise amplified the otherwise heavy silence that filled the neglected space.

He began his task, photographing the first floor, noting that the corridor doors were all damaged, some lying on the ground. The area was permeated by strong odours of damp, mould, and what could only be described as the smell of the men's toilet.

Notice boards had been ripped from the walls and thrown into otherwise empty rooms. In one room, a metal bed frame had been turned onto its side, melted candle wax still present on its surface. Graffiti in red spray paint reading *"The devil lives here"* and *"Dead angels don't cry"* was visible on the walls, alongside empty beer cans, cigarette butts, and broken glass littering the floor.

The corridor was dimly lit, with only faint light filtering through cracked and broken window panes, dirt and moss growing in the gaps.

Each step echoed off the battered tiles, amplifying the oppressive silence. He passed faded remnants of old posters from the health service. Layers of dust, plaster, and fragments of broken glass crunched beneath his boots as he moved carefully, glancing at the exposed wiring that hung loosely from the walls and ceiling.

As George proceeded upstairs, he heard the wind moving debris, creating sounds reminiscent of footsteps within the stairwell or the corridor. The upper corridor smelled of burnt wood and paper, with all the doors forcefully detached and scattered along the floor. Discarded soft drink and beer cans, along with food wrappers, were abundant. The metal beds were absent, leaving each room vacant except for one, which contained two orange plastic chairs—one of which was partially melted. George took several photos, glanced around each room briefly, and then decided to move to the next floor.

The staircase was littered with window blinds, old sheets, and piles of blank medical paperwork, dust motes swirling in the pale shafts of sunlight. Shadows danced along the walls as he navigated around piles of rubble and broken bed frames. He noticed that each room had been stripped of all contents, including copper piping and even the radiators. Charred marks streaked across the floors near several doorways, hinting at past fires. The silence was punctuated only by the distant clatter of loose roof tiles rattling in the breeze.

Upon reaching the end of the corridor, George checked his phone—11:53. He estimated he would complete his task within a couple more hours. He took a few more photos of the corridor and stairwell, then paused briefly, wiping perspiration from his brow, only to feel a chill settle against his skin. The hollow echo of dripping water underscored the eerie emptiness. Where once there might have been signs of life—laughter, conversation, warmth—now only the occasional scurry of a rat in the walls or the flicker of movement in the corner of his eye offered any semblance of activity. Throughout, George remained attentive, methodically cataloguing every scar left upon the building by time, neglect, and misuse.

After about an hour, he arrived at the fourth floor. The corridor in this section was narrower, marked by yellow tape with black stripes, accompanied by a sign that read, *Keep Out*. George ducked under the tape, then checked the camera battery, which remained strong. He looked down the corridor, which appeared darker than the others.

The walls were painted in shades of emerald green, and the floor featured pale yellow tiles, some of which were loose, exposing concrete beneath. Several tiles had been displaced further down the corridor. At the far end, there was an overturned wooden bench with three metal trolleys stacked on top of each other.

As George proceeded down the corridor, he paused occasionally to take some photos, verifying that the lighting was sufficient. The subdued illumination cast an ominous atmosphere, and the cooler air carried subtle hints of body odour and a tangy, musty smell.

His steps resounded quietly against the concrete floor, punctuated by the sporadic noise of a shifting tile. He came across an unmarked brown wood-effect door with a silver handle, and someone had stuck a pencil into the keyhole. He pulled on the handle and found the door unlocked. Upon opening it, George discovered it was a small cleaning cupboard containing three shelves, all empty except for the bottom shelf, which had several rags and a few rusty ring marks.

As he was about to close the door, George noticed four old Polaroid photos pinned to it. Each image displayed blurred faces, likely the result of motion. The presence of these photos in a cleaning cupboard struck him as unusual. Nevertheless, he simply closed the door and continued taking more photos.

The quietness felt almost oppressive—relieved only by the occasional call of a herring gull somewhere outside. Dust motes floated through the limited rays of light entering from both ends of the corridor, while cobwebs accumulated near the ceiling corners. Every door was secured with a thick steel chain and padlock, the chains drilled into the walls beside each door frame and looped through the door. The exception was Room 31, where the chain hung loosely from the handle and the door was slightly ajar.

As George approached Room 31, he noticed scratches around the doorframe, accompanied by stains of a dark substance—potentially dried blood. A slight draft emerged from beneath the door, shifting fragments of debris across the floor.

George felt an unusual sensation in his chest as his heart rate increased. This wasn't fear, but rather a sense of apprehension—a feeling that resembled entering into a memory he did not consciously recall. Standing outside Room 31, he paused to compose himself, placed his hand on the door, and proceeded to open it carefully.

As the door creaked on its hinges, a faint smell of disinfectant greeted him—a mix of dust and something metallic lingered in the air. The temperature inside the room was noticeably colder, with sunlight filtering through a barred window, casting narrow stripes of pale light across the floor.

Beneath the window sat a metal bedframe, devoid of its mattress, its springs exposed and rusted in places. The corners of the room were shadowy, barely illuminated except where the sunlight fell.

Above a smashed porcelain washbasin, a small, round mirror hung, fractured down the centre, splintering George's reflection into jagged pieces. As he stepped further into the room, the crunch of broken tiles and fallen plaster underfoot made every movement seem amplified, echoing against the stark emptiness of the room, making the hairs on his arm rise. The walls were marred by extensive areas of peeling paint, curling away from the plaster like old paper, revealing patches of faded green beneath.

He looked around the room, assessing optimal vantage points for his photographs. Raising his camera, he pressed the shutter, noting how loud the click was in the otherwise silent room. Upon reviewing the image on the preview screen, he was momentarily taken aback. Contrary to his initial impression, the room was not empty. Six figures stood—gaunt and eerily composed—in hospital gowns frayed at the edges, some stained and threadbare. Their feet were bare against the broken tiles, toes curled in silent anticipation. Their smiles were unsettling—not joyful, but fixed, as if rehearsed, with eyes that glimmered with an intensity suggesting stories left untold. He could see a wristband slipping down one man's arm, the faded ink barely legible. Despite the warmth in their expressions, the atmosphere vibrated with quiet tension, making him hesitate before lowering the camera.

George glanced upward and methodically searched the room. The pale afternoon light filtered through the window, casting shadows on the peeling paint and dust-laden tiled concrete floor. However, the room was vacant; he was the sole occupant. The air felt heavy with stillness, amplifying the distant cries of the herring gulls outside.

George examined the photograph once more. The six figures remained in place, their smiles unnervingly broad and their eyes unnaturally reflective, glinting as if catching a hidden source of light. Details that seemed insignificant—creases in their hospital gowns, faint patterns on the painted walls behind them—appeared disturbingly sharp. One individual, a tall bald man, seemed to be concealing an object behind his back. His posture suggested he was turning slightly away from the group, his shadow merging with the edge of the frame.

Dismissing the anomaly as a technical issue, George reasoned that it could be an image overlay from the camera's memory card or a reflection from the window bars causing shadows to resemble people. He proceeded to take another photo. As he raised the camera, his fingers hesitated for a moment over the shutter release—a fleeting chill racing up his spine despite his rational explanations.

There were now seven individuals present. It appeared an additional person had joined the group. The familiar faces and expressions remained unchanged—eyes either averted or locked in silent communication. Shadows stretched across the dimly lit room, lending an air of mystery and claustrophobia. The tall man continued to withhold something from view.

Without using the viewfinder, George captured a third photo. His breath shallow, he pressed the shutter. He glanced down at the camera's display, heart pounding, and reviewed the image with growing unease.

This time, there were eight individuals visible—sharper outlines, positioned closer than before, almost overlapping. Their features seemed subtly altered—eyes wider, mouths tightened—and a sudden sense of intrusion filled the space.

Cold perspiration formed along the back of his neck, creeping under his collar. The hairs on his arms stood on end, and every sound in the room felt amplified—the quiet broken only by the distant dripping of water and the muted rustle of clothing. Uncertainty gnawed at him as he tried to convince himself that what he saw was simply a trick of the light—or the product of his imagination.

He retreated into the corridor, hoping to exit the room unaccompanied. However, there was a subtle change in the corridor. The paint on the walls appeared slightly darker, and a faint odour of disinfectant lingered in the air. The overhead lights swayed gently in the breeze, casting uneasy shadows that danced across the floor. His footsteps echoed louder than usual, as if the space had grown emptier.

He proceeded to complete his task across the remainder of the corridor. Upon reviewing the photographs, he noticed that each photo—including those captured at each end of the corridor and stairwell—featured the figures from Room 31. The faces were unmistakable. Their eyes seemed oddly luminous, and they consistently displayed smiles that stretched wider in every subsequent frame, until the expression bordered on unnatural. The figures were not stationary; they appeared to be inching closer, looming towards him.

By the time he arrived at the stairwell, the number of individuals depicted had increased to ten. Their presence grew more claustrophobic—some faces almost pressed against the lens, others peering over the shoulders of others or crowding the periphery.

When he reached the fifth floor, a strange odour mixed disinfectant and stale cigarette smoke. The air felt damp and slightly colder against his skin. His boots made faint squeaking sounds on the uneven dark blue tiles, some chipped at the corners. This level consisted of office rooms—smashed doors hung open or tilted at strange angles, their nameplates faded from years of neglect. Some pigeons were present, likely having entered through broken windows, their feathers leaving trails of dust and debris as they flapped, startled by his presence. There were piles of papers and broken coffee mugs scattered across the floor.

As George entered one of the offices, he heard a metallic click behind him, echoing off the walls. He turned around, his heartbeat quickening, and raised his camera, ready to capture whatever moved in the silence—but saw nothing. Just empty space, marked by scattered office chairs and toppled filing cabinets.

He continued walking, each step muted by nervous anticipation. Then he heard another click, this time so soft it seemed almost imagined, blending into the distant cooing of the pigeons and the low hum of distant traffic outside.

He realised with a creeping unease that it was the exact sound of his camera's shutter.

He forced himself to continue working, recognising that despite his growing apprehension, the money for this assignment would help settle outstanding bills. Each shutter click felt heavier than usual, as if the shadows themselves pressed in closer with every passing minute.

Nevertheless, the persistent sensation of being watched remained unsettling. It grew sharper when the room fell quiet, and the only sounds were the whispering drafts rustling papers across the floor.

Occasionally, while looking through the viewfinder, he perceived what sounded like faint, rhythmic breathing—distinctly not his own. The cadence of the breaths was subtle but unmistakable, rising and falling just beyond his line of sight, causing a chill to prickle along the back of his neck. Every so often, he would pause his work to peer into the gloom behind him, half expecting to catch a glimpse of someone lurking at the edge of his vision. But each time, there was only stillness and a deepening unease.

In an office adjacent to the stairwell, he discovered a filing cabinet pushed onto its side, its metal drawers gaping open, and their contents spilled in a chaotic fan of paperwork across the scuffed tiled floor. The scent of musty old paper and damp seemed to hang in the air. He stepped carefully through the mess, the soles of his boots crunching softly on scattered staples, paperclips, and torn folders. He picked up a handful of papers and thumbed through them. Then his heart skipped a beat.

PATIENT RECORD 038832: Crouch, G.

Date of Admission: 12th April 1958

Notes: The patient was brought in by the local constabulary due to concerns regarding his well-being. He exhibited behaviour consistent with attempting to interact physically with individuals who were not present. The patient reports beliefs of being a time traveller.

Severe dissociation and persistent visual hallucinations observed. Isolation recommended.

Upon further evaluation by Dr. Rice, Mr. Crouch engaged in continuous conversations with invisible entities and attempted to open doors for absent persons. He described detailed experiences of travelling through different eras, insisting that certain staff members resembled people he had met in past centuries. The patient demonstrated confusion about current events and appeared disoriented regarding temporal references, frequently referencing dates and locations unrelated to reality.

Auditory hallucinations were indicated by his response to voices others could not hear. Initial assessment suggested acute psychosis with possible underlying schizoaffective disorder. Treatment options under consideration include antipsychotic medication and structured therapeutic activities.

Staff are advised to maintain clear boundaries and minimise environmental stressors to reduce exacerbation of symptoms.

Attached to the form was a black-and-white patient photo. The male in the photo was unmistakably himself—identical bone structure, a distinct scar above the left eyebrow—though several decades younger.

He squinted at the photo, studying each detail—the curve of the smile, the intensity behind the eyes. Unease prickled his skin. Reading the document again, his hand exhibited a slight tremor, the edge of the paper fluttering between his fingers as uncertainty clouded his mind. He placed the paper down on the filing cabinet and exited the office promptly, glancing over his shoulder as if half-expecting someone—or something—to follow him.

George decided to return to Room 31. He hesitated at the threshold of the room, the stale corridor pressing in on him. Something gnawed at him, an unfinished urge, and he decided he needed one last photo. Just one more.

The moment he stepped inside, the air shifted. It felt much colder now—unnaturally so. His breath coiled in front of him like smoke, drifting toward the far corner. The silence was oppressive, broken only by the herring gulls calling to each other outside.

His fingers stiffened as he raised the camera. The plastic of the shutter button bit into his skin, as though frozen to the touch. He swallowed hard, steadied himself, and clicked.

Then the image appeared on the preview screen—George's stomach lurched.

Twelve figures. They stood together in a semicircle—pale and rigid, their faces warped with grief and malice. But this time, something was wrong—horribly wrong.

In the middle of them was him.

George's heart hammered against his ribs, each beat like a fist on a coffin lid. His vision blurred as panic surged. He stumbled backward into the doorframe, gripping it so hard the wood creaked. The air carried a sharper tang now—bleach, disinfectant, rot—fumes thick enough to claw at his throat. He gagged, coughed, and the taste of chemicals stung his tongue.

His gaze darted around the room, wild and desperate. The peeling paint seemed to pulse. The shadows seemed to lean closer.

How could he be in the photograph?

And more importantly, who had taken it?

Just then, a sharp click broke the silence. George froze, his fingers hovering nowhere near the shutter. He hadn't taken the picture. Slowly, he looked up. Another click—this time followed by a blinding flash. His vision washed white, and for a moment, he was lost in the glare.

When his sight returned, the world was different. He was no longer apart from the figures—he was among them. The cold was inside him now, seeping through his skin, settling deep into his bones.

As one of them, the others turned their heads toward him. Their fixed grins unwavering, eyes glinting with something that wasn't human.

The tall man stepped forward. His hand—ice-cold and heavy—

rested on George's shoulder. Slowly, he pressed something into George's palm.

George looked down. A camera.

The tall man's smile widened as he whispered—almost tenderly—

"Welcome, George. We've missed you."

Four days later, a group of urban explorers slipped through the asylum's broken doors. The building groaned with silence, its corridors suffocating with mildew and the sweet, metallic tang of rust.

In one of the upper rooms, they discovered a camera lying in the dust. One of the explorers knelt down to pick it up. The floor was thick with grime, but what struck them was how untouched it seemed—no footprints, no signs of disturbance—as if the camera had rested there for decades, waiting.

They turned it on.

The first image showed twelve figures standing in that very room, draped in faded hospital gowns. Their skin looked grey and papery, stretched too thin over hollow frames. Most faced the camera with stiff, unnatural smiles—their teeth bared like masks. But in the centre stood a man who did not smile. His mouth hung slack, a line of drool glistening at his chin. His eyes rolled back until only the whites stared forward— luminous and wrong.

They scrolled further.

The walls behind the figures were mottled with peeling paint and streaked with symbols traced in a dark, rust-like crust. With each photo, the shadows deepened—unnaturally sharp, cutting across the painted walls despite the dim light. The shapes clung to the figures like living things, stretching longer and darker—as though the camera had captured not the absence of light, but something hungry.

And always, the man at the centre. His blank expression did not change. Around his wrist gleamed a hospital bracelet, stamped with numbers blurred beyond recognition, as if the lens recoiled from revealing them.

Then came the final photograph.

The explorers leaned closer, their breath fogging the screen. The twelve figures remained, but their faces had been blurred into formless smears, melting into nothing. All but one. At the centre, his face was sharp. Too sharp. His eyes locked onto the lens with dreadful clarity, and though they knew it was impossible, every one of them felt it at once:

He was no longer looking at the camera. He was looking at them.

Chapter 5
Adenburge

The year was 1348.

Mist settled over the thatched roofs of Adenburge, a small village you would not find on any maps today. Chickens and goats moved through the mud in the village square, but there was no visible activity involving feeding. Doors were open, but there was no movement across the thresholds.

In the early morning, a gentle mist rolled through the winding lanes, kind of obscuring the old, faded signposts and giving a softer look to the weather-beaten timber homes. You could catch a whiff of damp earth mingling with something almost heavy—a hint of decay, mixed with a strong scent of wood smoke wafting from faraway fireplaces. It was a strange combination, really—both comforting and a little eerie at the same time. In the center, dishevelled chickens pecked listlessly at puddles and bare floors, their feathers streaked with mud and clay. Not one villager stirred; the silence was broken only by the intermittent, deep resonant croak of a raven perched atop a sagging fence. Shadows pooled in empty doorways, as if the lives within had momentarily slipped away, leaving only the silent heartbeat of Adenburge's stillness.

The church tower's bell had remained silent for a few weeks. In the village square, its absence was unnerving—a constant reminder of lives lost and rituals left undone.

Father Baines, the priest, was found deceased in his bed, his darkened lips and his rosary entwined in his hands. His passing left a palpable void in the community; the faithful gathered at his door, but no one dared approach too closely. His remains, like many of the others, had not been interred. The graveyard overflowed, unattended, as the gravediggers themselves succumbed to the illness or died in fear. The plague arrived rapidly, beginning with coughing and fever, followed by the appearance of dark swellings on the body that would rupture. Within days, entire households fell ill, their homes marked with hastily painted symbols warning others to stay away. Precautionary measures included mothers covering their children's faces with cloth soaked in vinegar, men wearing sprigs of lavender in their clothing, hoping its scent would ward off the "bad air." Food and supplies grew scarce as merchants ceased visiting, and silence settled over the lanes and the village square, broken only by the distant moans and cries of the afflicted. The whispered prayers received no apparent response, and hope gradually faded from even the most devout villagers' eyes.

By late spring, the graveyard was overrun. There were too many dead. Shallow pits were dug in the village square itself, bodies thrown in by the few survivors who still had the strength to lift or drag them. Lime was scarce. The stench of rotting flesh clung to every beam and stone.

Then the voices began—just one or two at first, but after a few days, there were more and more.

Those who lingered told of whispers at night, a rasping chorus that drifted on the wind. They claimed to hear fingernails scratching on the doors of their homes—soft at first, then furious. One widower swore he heard his wife, dead three days, calling to him from the window. When he looked, he saw her—her mouth sewn shut with dark swellings, her eyes wet with black tears.

No one came to save them. The world beyond Adenburge turned its back. Rumours spread that the village had been cursed by its own. That in their last moments of agony, the dying had called out not to any saint, but to something older, darker.

By the time winter came, silence fell. The remaining villagers— those who could still walk—left, walking into the woods and leaving everything behind. Bread on the tables, fires still burning in the hearths. Cradles rocking empty in the breeze.

Over time, trees gradually reclaimed the lanes and the homes. Roots forced their way through the floors of the houses and barns, while leaves swept over abandoned doorways. Roofs deteriorated and eventually collapsed, enclosing empty rooms to the elements, as snow and wind accelerated the decay. A violent storm struck, causing the ancient church tower—a local landmark—to crumble into ruins. By the beginning of the new century, only moss-covered stones littered the landscape, and skeletal remains lay scattered beneath the square, silent witnesses to what once was.

Adenburge village just kind of slipped away from people's memories over time. It's like there's no record of it anymore, and locals don't really mention it. Those old maps? They faded into obscurity. And the stories? Well, they've become pretty murky. Even the people who live in the next village hardly bring it up anymore. It's as if Adenburge has become a ghost of the past. The prevailing sentiment held that the area was devoid of sanctity—a place where blessings would never reach.

Nevertheless, those interred there remained in their graves, marked by plague and unrest. Leathered headstones stood askew, wild grass tangled around them. Uneasy legends circulated among travellers, suggesting restless spirits lingered, unable to find peace beneath the haunted soil.

Farley Meadow, 2017

Centuries later, the land had become little more than a stretch of tangled woodland—unremarkable and largely forgotten. Rabbits and foxes now made their burrows where once people had walked and lived.

Then a housing association purchased the plot at a low price. Developers swiftly moved in, clearing the trees to make way for construction. Architects drew up the plans for three hundred new affordable homes.

By the autumn of 2017, the estate had a name: Farley Meadow. Rows of identical grey-brick houses lined the streets, each with a neat driveway gleaming faintly beneath the weak sun. Railings stood where the woods had once been, and marketing banners declared with cheerful optimism: "A fresh bright start in the countryside."

The first families arrived, keys jingling, bright smiles. They marvelled at the quiet—no more loud traffic, no neighbours yet. A blank canvas for new lives.

Yet the workers who had broken the ground whispered differently. They remembered the things they'd found—rows and rows of bones, blackened and brittle, packed tightly together. One labourer swore he dug up a crude mask, clinging to the roots of an oak tree, its hollow eyes staring. The foreman ordered it all to be removed—quietly dumped, paperwork unsigned.

"You don't need to tell anyone about this; it'll only cause delays, and then you lot won't get your bonus." The foreman moaned, looking around at all the workers. "Anyway, it's old rubbish from the 1920s. They must've had a Halloween party up here and left it all behind. That's all it is." He turned and went back to his office.

Every living soul may have forgotten Adenburge, but the land still remembered.

On the first night, the Carter family sat in their spotless lounge, boxes stacked high, Caddo boxes scattered across the floor.

Sarah Carter, mother of two, laughed about the silence outside. "It's like living in the middle of nowhere. Beautiful peace," she said, smiling at David.

Her husband, David, nodded. "Exactly what we want. No more city life for the Carter family." He said cheerfully.

Upstairs, their youngest, Kallie, stood at her window. She could see the dark field where the last house hadn't been finished yet. The grass swayed strangely in the wind, patterns that seemed too deliberate, like shapes forming and then breaking apart.

"Daddy," she called down, "there are strange things out there." When David came up, there was nothing—only a half-finished house and a pale moon.

Across the estate, other families settled in. Lights blinked on, families watching televisions in their new homes. All was good, but in the quiet hours just before dawn, when the houses should have been still, strange things stirred.

Shadows crossed the streets where no one had walked. A damp, sour smell drifted on the breeze, seeping through open windows. And in the soil behind each garden fence, something shifted—something restless.

Beneath the driveway and foundations, the dead villagers of Adenburge stirred.

The first few weeks passed without incident. David and Sarah Carter unpacked. Then the Jenkins family moved next door to the Carters. The Jenkins spent their first week planting shrubs and roses in the front garden. Farley Meadow began to look alive.

Then, one night, the noises began.

Sarah Carter was awoken by scratching. Faint at first, she thought it was a mouse that had climbed into the walls. But when she pressed her ear to the wall, it seemed to move—upward, downward, side to side—as though something was scratching patterns from within.

David dismissed it. "New builds, always make noises. Pipes settling, or the floors maybe settling, or it could be a rat stuck in the wall."

But Sarah had noticed Kallie had started to sleep on the floor of her brother's room, clutching her teddy tightly.

"Kallie doesn't like her window," said twelve-year-old Jack.

When Sarah asked Kallie about her window, Kallie whispered… "They tap on it. Every night."

Other houses felt it too. Mrs. Baven, two doors down, complained of a smell in her kitchen—rancid and fleeting—gone before she could find the source.

The Jenkins family had problems as well. Their dog would bark and growl at unseen things in most of the rooms in the house. Its hackles would rise and then back off—still growling.

After the noises came the shadows.

Streetlamps would dim and then glow stronger, casting long shadows that stretched too far across the road and pavement. Mr. O'Malley swore he saw three figures moving between the unfinished houses—men stooped, their faces hidden, their strides broken, like joints bending wrong.

Then, when he shone his torch across the plots, there was nothing but scaffolding, just emptiness.

By the third week, unease had taken root. Neighbours whispered to each other on their driveways, trading stories with nervous laughter that rang hollow.

Farley Meadow

2017

The construction crew digging a trench for a drainage system struck something unusual. The digger's claw churned up what appeared to be a pit—shallow and broad. The foreman cursed when he realised it wasn't empty. A tangled mass of bones, blackened by age, emerged from the earth, with soil clinging to the fractured skulls.

One worker gagged. "That's not normal burial. They've been... tossed in."

The foreman barked out orders, his voice sharp and quick. "Fill it, seal it, and divert the drainage system around it. And most of all, don't say anything. The housing project has deadlines to meet and investors' promises to keep. Now, get back to work."

But the smell lingered that evening—thick and cloying, carried by the wind to every home. A stench of decaying flesh and rotting cloth, left to mildew. And as the streetlights blinked into life, every family heard it. A whispering chorus, faint and raspy, drifting through the streets. It sounded like words, though none in any living tongue.

Kallie Carter pressed her face into her pillow, her eyes shut tightly.

From outside her window came a gentle tapping.

Not with knuckles. Not with stones. With nails—long, yellowed fingernails.

Sarah Carter couldn't sleep. The noises had grown worse—scratching, tapping, and now whispers. They were so faint, she could almost believe they were in her own head.

David insisted it was stress. "You're just overtired, love. New home, new job, kids unsettled. Believe me, it will soon pass."

But it wasn't passing.

One morning, after David left for work and Jack had trudged off to school, Sarah sat in the kitchen and opened her laptop at the breakfast bar. She typed in "The Farley Meadow development history." Nothing. Only glossy promotional material—drone shots of neat brick homes and rolling countryside.

Frustrated, she widened her search: old maps, local archives, parish records. That's when she saw it… a name buried deep in a scanned manuscript from the 17th century. Adenburge.

She frowned, zooming in. The handwriting was cramped, the ink faded, but the description chilled her blood.

"…the village of Adenburge, hollowed by pestilence, abandoned, and left to rot. Here, the bodies lay unshriven, piled in pits without prayer nor sacrament. Locals speak of Adenburge, where the dead scratch at doors and whisper through the reeds. The priest himself was taken, leaving no blessing. God's grace departed this place."

Sarah leaned back on her stool. Adenburge, she said quietly to herself.

She pulled up an old map overlay and felt her throat tighten. The new housing project, Farley Meadow, sat squarely on the faint markings of the forgotten village. The cluster of streets matched the rough layout of where cottages had once stood. The field where houses had yet to be built was the old square, where the plague pits had been dug. The kitchen seemed suddenly colder. A faint but sharp smell drifted through the room, rising in her nostrils… damp earth and the stench of rot.

Sarah slammed the laptop shut.

From upstairs, she heard Kallie's small voice. Not calling her—just talking. Soft, low, as though answering someone she shouldn't.

When Sarah climbed the stairs, she found her daughter sitting on her small chair by the window, her face pale, eyes fixed on the glass. Her teddy lay limp in her lap.

"Kallie, sweetheart," Sarah whispered, "Who are you talking to?"

Her daughter turned around slowly, her voice flat, as if repeating the words given to her.

"They say we don't belong here. They say this was their village first." And then, as though realising she'd said too much, Kallie buried her face in the teddy's fur and began to cry.

Sarah looked around the room, then comforted Kallie.

By late November, frost rimmed the windows, and half-built houses at the far end of the street stood like black teeth against the sky. Families decorated their windows with paper stars and glowing reindeer, but the cheer seemed thin, as though smothered by the land beneath. Mrs. Broad, who lived opposite the Carters, swore her dining room clock ticked backwards for a full three minutes before being flung off the shelf and shattering as it hit the carpet.

Mr. and Mrs. Oawa found muddy handprints on their bathroom and bedroom walls—high up, near the ceiling, where no child could reach.

And Sarah noticed that the smell had some kind of routine. It wasn't constant; it came in waves. Damp earth, rotting flesh, the iron tang of blood, wafting through the estate every couple of nights.

Kallie no longer wanted to draw flowers and rainbows in her doodle books. Her drawings grew darker each day, gaunt figures with swollen faces, the flesh covered in red and circular spots, their arms dragged too long, ending in claws that scratched the edges of the paper.

Their mouths gaped wide, full of black teeth and what seemed to be worms.

One night, as Sarah asked about the figures in Kallie's drawing, her daughter's eyes went glassy. The crayon slipped from her hand and landed near the door.

"They show me how," Kallie whispered, her eyes shifting to the window. **"They tell me what comes next. We can't hide."**

In the next bedroom, Jack grew restless, waking up to cough until his throat bled. Sarah had taken him to the doctor, but the doctor found no infection.

"It's probably down to stress," the doctor said.

Other parents on the street noticed that their children were starting to get coughing fits, sudden fevers, and strange rashes that bloomed overnight but faded by morning. The sickness seemed to spread quietly from house to house.

It was on one of those uneasy, wind-chilled nights that Sarah heard footsteps on the landing. Slow, dragging shuffles and a muffled humming. She rose from her bed, her heart pounding, and slowly opened the bedroom door, peering into the cold hallway. Shadows shifted in the dim light. Jack's door was ajar, his coughing muffled under his duvet.

On the stairs, a shape lingered. For a moment, Sarah thought she saw a little girl—thin, with hair plastered to a grey brow, her eyes feverishly bright. But as Sarah reached out to touch the child, she dissolved into mist, leaving only the stale smell of damp earth and a faint, childish giggle echoing down the staircase.

Sarah slowly backed into her bedroom, shutting the door quietly with trembling hands. She pressed her back against it, as if trying to keep something out.

David stirred in the bed, half-asleep.

"What's the matter?" he mumbled, sitting up and rubbing his eyes.

She wanted to tell him everything—that Jack was much sicker, that Kallie was talking to unseen figures in her bedroom, that she herself was seeing things that couldn't be explained. She walked toward the bed but tried to speak, only for her voice to get caught in her throat. Instead, she whispered, **"There's someone in the house."**

David's attention sharpened. He sat up on the edge of the bed and listened, but the house seemed quiet. He grabbed a golf club from the corner of the room and crept into the dim hallway. Nothing. Only the faint creak of the floorboards beneath his feet.

By morning, Sarah told herself she had imagined it, but Jack's coughing grew worse. Kallie refused to leave her room, standing by the window, staring at the patch of land where the unfinished houses still stood.

The Carter family wasn't the only one suffering.

Mr. Oawa was found in his T-shirt and shorts, asleep in the backyard at four in the morning, soaked through with dew. When his wife shook him awake, he swore he had been speaking to his late brother, though the man had been dead for twenty years.

Mr. and Mrs. Jenkins found their dog dead at the foot of the stairs, its lips pulled back in a deathly snarl, as if it had faced something no one else could see. The house had been silent... then suddenly, Billyboy was just there, dead.

The smell returned, heavier each night. It no longer drifted in slowly, but pressed in—thick and rancid, soaking curtains, carpets, and cushions. No matter how many times they washed the curtains and tried to freshen up the carpet, the stench stayed.

Sarah sat again at her laptop, desperate. She typed the name Adenburge into every archive, every online record she could find. But most results were blank. Pages refused to load, links dissolved into error messages. The few documents she managed to open spoke of the same thing: the cursed village of Adenburge, the cursed earth, and late-night whispers for those who venture near what was once Adenburge.

The handwritten account chilled her the most. It was from the priest of the nearby village...

The sickness did not end with the dying.

Those unshriven would not rest in their graves. The pestilence bred voices, and the voices bred forms. What had once been living souls now walked again, but in ruin. They were called back—not by God, but by their own hunger. It is said they will return, should their resting place be disturbed in any way.

Sarah slammed the laptop shut once more.

That night, the tapping at Kallie's window grew louder and louder. Sarah rushed into her daughter's room and threw open the curtains. Outside, in the frost-slick grass of the garden, stood dozens of figures. They did not move, did not breathe. They were mottled and bloated, their limbs twisted, their mouths yawning wide in silent, black chants.

And though they were yards away, Sarah heard them as clearly as if they were in the room—a chorus of whispers: "You have awoken us. We will not be forgotten."

Kallie stood beside her now, no longer afraid, her voice flat and calm.

"Mummy," she said, taking hold of Sarah's hand, "they told me. They told me all. The plague never left. It only sleeps. And now we have awoken them up."

Sarah yanked the curtains shut and dragged Kallie away from the window. But the whispering didn't stop. It seemed to seep through the glass, through the very walls, the words scratching like rusted nails across her bones.

In the next room, Jack was coughing again—violently, choking, until he retched dark, wet clots that stained his sheets. Sarah screamed for David, who ran upstairs two steps at a time. But as he burst into Jack's room, his face drained of colour.

Jack was not alone.

A thin, grey, bony hand rested on Jack's shoulder. Its fingers were long—too long—and its nails black and split. A face leaned down toward Jack's face, a face David recognised from a dream he had—lips sewn shut, skin swollen with plague, red lumps dotting the surface. The moment David swung his fist, the figure dissolved into mist, leaving only the stench of rotten flesh and a trail of muddy handprints across the wall.

That night, every family on Farley Meadow awoke to the same thing:

Knocking on their windows.

Whispers in every room.

Gentle at first. Then furious.

Glass cracked. Curtains billowed, though windows stayed shut. Children wailed. Dogs howled. And then, the ground itself groaned and shifted, like it was breathing.

The unfinished houses at the end of the street buckled, then crumbled into the mud. The earth shifted, swelling, then splitting open as though something beneath was clawing upwards. A stench poured out so thick and foul that it made the air almost unbearable. Figures clambered from the pits—dozens, then hundreds—dragging themselves free. Their bones snapped as they straightened. Their eyes glistened with black tears.

They did not rush. They did not stumble. They walked—slow and steady, toward the houses.

David shouted to Sarah to get Kallie and Jack while he got the car ready. Doors swung open across the estate as families spilled into the streets, all staring in the same direction—the plague pit, overflowing with the dead, climbing over one another to escape the pit. And then darkness. Every light went out.

Not just the streetlights. Not just the houses.

Everything.

Even the moon and stars seemed to blink away, not wanting to see what had come. Leaving only darkness and the sound of shuffling feet.

Whispers drifted on the breeze through the darkness, closer and closer, inside everyone's ears...

"You built upon our bones, you breathed our air. You lived where our houses once stood. You are now with us. You can't leave. Soon, you will be one of us."

Sarah clutched Kallie close, desperate to feel the warmth of her daughter's body. But when she looked down, her stomach twisted. Kallie wasn't holding on. She stood rigid, her spine unnaturally straight, her small frame suddenly alien. Her little hand slid from Sarah's grip like dead weight.

"Mummy," Kallie whispered. Her lips shaped the word, but the sound that followed was not hers.

It was layered—an endless chorus, deep and high all at once, voices that seemed to come from somewhere deep within. Then Kallie started humming. A thousand unseen throats joined her.

The air thickened, and the stench of rotten flesh flooded everyone's nostrils.

Kallie lifted her face and smiled at Sarah. Sarah recoiled. Her daughter's teeth had blackened into jagged stones, her eyes clouded into blank, white orbs. Her smile stretched wider than her cheeks should allow.

Jack doubled over, retching blood in great, wet gulps. His coughs turned to convulsions, his chest heaving unnaturally, ribs bulging as if something beneath pressed against the bone.

Then, at last, he stilled. His head snapped upright with a loud crack. And then he started smiling. His lips split open, blood pouring freely, but the grin remained, carved into his face.

Across the estate, windows flickered with frantic, brief shadows. Screams erupted—then ceased abruptly, cut short, and silence followed. But the silence lasted only moments before the air thickened with laughter.

But it was no human laughter. It gurgled wetly, inhumanly, from every house all at once, a perfect unison that trembled the glass in Sarah's windows.

She saw them through the mist… neighbours twisting, their bones bending like wax, their skin blotched with black, splitting as something cold and rotting writhed beneath it. Mouths opened too wide, lips tearing, and what spilled from their eyes was no longer theirs.

The truth cracked through Sarah's mind then, unbearable: The plague had never been a sickness. It was a hunger.

The dead had returned. They had been waiting for vessels to rise.

By dawn, Farley Meadow was silent. The estate stood like a corpse, stripped clean. Homes gutted, gardens churned as though plowed by vast unseen hands, fences torn down as if gnawed. Cars sat askew, doors yawning wide, headlights still burning through the fog. Not a single body remained, not a trace of the people who had laughed, cooked, and lived there.

Only the faint sound lingered in the fog—a twisted echo of children's voices, reciting in a tongue that scraped against the mind, a language too vast and old for human throats.

And beneath it all, the steady pulse of something vast and patient, still feeding, still waiting—as though the land itself was breathing again for the first time in centuries.

The smell still remained, a heavy, suffocating stench of plague and death that never lifted again.

The Aftermath

By January, Farley Meadow was empty.

Estate agents stopped taking calls. The developers pulled the website. Police tape fluttered on broken fences, but no one patrolled. The neat rows of houses stood silent, windows dark, doors ajar, driveways littered with abandoned belongings, and cars half-parked as if their owners had meant to return.

Locals from nearby towns whispered about the place, but none dared go near. Some swore they saw shapes moving behind the curtains, pale faces staring from upstairs windows. Others said the mist never cleared, even when the rest of the countryside basked in bright sunshine.

Months later, a pair of surveyors came to assess the site. They didn't last an hour. When they staggered back to the main road, their boots caked in mud, their faces were grey, hollow-eyed. They refused to speak of what they'd seen, save for a single word one of them muttered under his breath...

"Adenburge."

Seasons turned. Grass grew long through the pavement, ivy clutching at the brickwork. Birds nested in the gutters. Farley Meadow sank into silence, as though it had never been lived in at all.

And then, years later, another sign appeared. A fresh banner stretched across the roadside:

COMING SOON – VALLEY DENE MODERN HOMES IN THE COUNTRYSIDE LIFESTYLE.

Another new beginning. Another blank canvas.

The land is waiting. Patiently waiting. Still hungry for more.

Chapter 6
Whispers for the Damned

Daniel's Tuesday began routinely: after showering and dressing, he would head to the kitchen, grab some toast and a glass of grapefruit juice just before leaving for work.

As part of his daily schedule, he stopped by his favourite shop, Style CoWee, to pick up his usual flat white. While standing in line and reading a few messages on his phone, he became aware of a faint whisper—barely audible, as if someone were speaking with their hand over their mouth. When Daniel turned around, there was no indication of anyone talking. The woman behind him was also on her phone texting, so it was not her.

The barista greeted him, stating, "Good morning, your usual?" Daniel nodded in response to the young woman behind the counter, placed his money on the counter, and then looked around the shop, attempting to identify the source of the whisper. He listened carefully, but the whisper had ceased.

As Daniel waited for his coffee, the gentle hum of conversation and the clinking of cups filled the air. The scent of freshly ground coffee beans mingled with traces of sweet pastries and bacon sandwiches, creating a comforting atmosphere that contrasted with the unease. He peered at the faces of the other customers, some buried in their phones, others quietly chatting, but nothing seemed suspicious or out of place.

With each passing second, the memory of the whisper grew more distant, yet a subtle prickle lingered at the back of his neck. Daniel found himself replaying the moment repeatedly in his mind, wondering whether stress or lack of sleep was making his imagination run wild. As he collected his coffee and thanked the barista, his gaze drifted once more to the shadowed corners of the coffee shop, searching for a clue that might explain what he had heard.

Daniel arrived at his office, still contemplating the source of the voice he had heard in the coffee shop. After taking his seat, he powered on his computer and began organising the paperwork that had been placed on his desk while waiting for the system to boot up.

As he drank his coffee, he briefly considered whether someone at the coffee shop had orchestrated a practical joke similar to those seen on television but ultimately set the thought aside and focused on his work responsibilities.

The office Daniel worked in was quiet, with only the hum of fluorescent lights overhead and the occasional shrill of a phone breaking the silence. Desks were neatly arranged in rows, computer monitors casting a pale blue glow across stacks of paperwork. A colleague walked past his cubicle, offered a brief nod, handed him a stack of documents, and politely asked him to review them by the end of the day.

The air was tinged with the robust aroma of freshly brewed coffee, mingling with the sharp scent of printer ink and the subtle trail of floral perfume left behind by passing coworkers. Outside, the distant rumble of traffic filtered through partially open windows, completing the familiar ambience of Daniel's daily routine.

Daniel methodically sorted through the paperwork, highlighting priority tasks in yellow. Occasionally, his gaze drifted to the window, staring at the clouds, replaying snatches of the morning's strange encounter, his brow furrowing in puzzlement. He shook off the distraction, tapping his fingers lightly on the desk, determined to tackle the day's agenda despite the lingering curiosity gnawing at the back of his mind.

Around lunchtime, Daniel was completing his morning tasks when he once again heard a whisper. This time it was slightly louder, although he still could not discern the message. He stood up quickly and looked around the office to determine if anyone noticed it, but his colleagues continued working, either talking on the phone or busy typing.

He noticed the sound recur three more times that same day, and by Friday, it was present every fifteen minutes. Sometimes it sounded the same, and other times the message seemed to change. Even in the office, the sound was audible while he was typing or when the phone rang, and it seemed to permeate all his activities.

The persistent noise followed him everywhere: muffled but unmistakable, echoing faintly in the quiet spaces between keystrokes and phone calls. Sometimes it grew louder in the late afternoon, as if responding to the waning daylight or the distant city traffic outside his window.

The voice was low, murmuring with a consistent rhythm, and he recognised that it was neither English, German, nor French. Its cadence carried hints of an ancient dialect, it seemed foreign yet oddly familiar, and now, each time he heard the whispers, goosebumps rose on his arms. Gradually, unease settled into his mind, making concentration difficult and sleep elusive. He found himself glancing over his shoulder and scanning empty corners of his place of work, wondering if anyone else could hear it.

Eventually, feeling both frustrated and increasingly concerned, Daniel activated the recording application on his phone to document the whispers. He decided to conduct the recording at home, where he felt most comfortable and the environment was quieter. He placed his phone carefully on the coffee table in front of him. However, upon playback, the recording contained only silence. No hint of any whispers, leaving him questioning his senses and searching for explanations in the quiet that followed.

At home, at work, and even out shopping, the whispers were with him all the time—during showers, meal times, everywhere. They seemed to come from every corner of the room, from the floorboards, lingering just at the edge of comprehension. Their sibilant tones blended with the hum of the refrigerator and the ticking of the clock, eroding any sense of normalcy.

Daniel now jolted awake at exactly 3:06 a.m. every morning, his sleep shattered by harrowing nightmares that grew more terrifying each night. In these dreams, he was trapped inside a glass coffin, helpless, as figures laughed at him. They pressed against the smooth surface, their eyes hollow with malice. Water seeped relentlessly into the coffin, rising inch by inch, chilling him to the bone as muted voices twisted into sinister chants. Each awakening left him gasping for air, tangled in drenched sheets, his heart pounding against his ribs like a drumbeat of panic. A sharp metallic tang stung his mouth while sinister, fragmented whispers echoed through his mind, just beyond comprehension.

Daniel's Growing Fear and Obsession with the Whispers:

Daniel had determined that the whispers were Latin, possibly a prayer or some kind of chant. The soft, rhythmic murmurs echoed through his mind, evoking memories of monastics singing, as their cadence closely resembled that of monks, each phrase rising and falling in sombre, harmonious waves. Daniel felt a chill creep along his spine as he listened, as though the whispers were drawing him in deeper into a world of ancient ritual and hidden meaning.

"Libera me, Domine, de morte aeterna, in die illa tremenda… quando caeli movendi sunt et terra.. dum veneris iudicare per ignem…"

Although Daniel was unfamiliar with Latin, the rhythm of the words unsettled him. He entered the phrase into an online translator for clarification.

"Deliver me, O Lord, from eternal death, on that awful day when the air is moved and the earth... when you come to judge the world by fire..."

Daniel's heart raced as the chilly silence was broken by solemn, trembling whispers that seemed to float through his flat. The cadence of the murmured words evoked ancient rituals, each syllable heavy with sorrow and reverence.

Confused and unsettled, Daniel strained to catch the meaning, his skin prickling as the chant ebbed and flowed around him like an invisible current. Why would he, alive and well, become the subject of such mournful prayers? He thought, still trying to make sense of the whispers.

As he listened to the whispered phrases, he noticed they were intended for him rather than directed at him. It suggested that unseen mourners expressed wishes for his deliverance or protection from an unspecified outcome. He understood that the prayer was meant to support him in dying peacefully.

He strained to catch the hushed voices around him, feeling the weight of each syllable as it drifted like incense through the lounge of his flat. Though he could not see the faces of those gathered, their presence was palpable; he knew they were there, watching and praying for him.

The words carried both hope and sorrow, intertwined — a plea not only for ease in his final days but also an unspoken yearning to shield him from whatever unknown fate awaited beyond the veil. The knowledge that these prayers were not rebukes but offerings of compassion filled him with a quiet acceptance, allowing him to surrender to the promise of a serene passage.

Daniel began to withdraw from his professional and social responsibilities, ceasing to attend work and isolating himself from others. He no longer responded to attempts at communication from friends and family. His once-structured life now slipped into a haze, as he retreated further into his thoughts, consumed by the whispers that refused to let go.

Subsequently, he started experiencing visual disturbances — seeing shadows and indistinct figures, such as nuns and priests, at the periphery of his vision. He also reported seeing individuals standing behind windows watching him or moving quickly into the hallway. On one occasion at the supermarket, as he reached for the fruit juice, he perceived a sensation of warm breath near his ear, accompanied by an urgent and intense voice:

"Requiem aeternam dona ei, Domine..."

"Did you hear that?" he asked a woman beside him. She turned her head slowly towards him, smiled, and then vanished.

Over the next few weeks, Daniel's withdrawal deepened; he often remained confined to his bedroom with the curtains drawn, showing little interest in personal hygiene or daily routines. Friends described him as increasingly restless and distracted, as if the world around him was becoming distant and unimportant.

Sleep eluded him entirely. He ensured every light in his flat remained on, arranging candles around his bed as a protective measure. He took additional precautions, including applying salt to windowsills, burning sage, and consulting with a priest.

Father Roberts responded with empathy, though he remained unconvinced by Daniel's concerns.

"You appear to be under considerable stress, Daniel. Perhaps you're doing too much overtime and not making time for yourself," Father Roberts advised. "Spiritual counselling or therapy might be beneficial."

That night, Daniel experienced a vivid dream of a mass grave, where innumerable bodies lay contorted in pain. Their flesh was rotten, and their hands were outstretched, trying to reach out to him. The scene was chilling, suffused with an overwhelming sense of decay. The whispering pervaded the scene, and soon the voices began to chant in Latin — a chorus of decaying mouths, intoning the same refrain:

"Danielus... Danielus... Dona eis requiem... Et lux perpetua luceateis..."

On a cold Saturday morning around three-thirty, Daniel woke up and made the impulsive decision to leave the city. Slipping out of bed, the silence of the pre-dawn hours hung heavily in the air. He didn't bother to pack; instead, he simply glanced around his flat, taking in all his worldly possessions, before moving quietly through the space, careful not to disturb the eerie stillness.

Once behind the wheel, Daniel hesitated for a moment. His breath fogged up the window as he started the engine. The city's streets lay deserted, cast in dim silver under the weight of the clouds overhead. Each streetlight flickered against the wet pavement, reflecting fleeting images of homes and shops he'd known for years.

As he drove further from his neighbourhood, memories began to surface—conversations with friends, laughter echoing in his favorite coffee shop—all muted by the distance and the closed doors behind him. A knot tightened in his stomach, uncertainty swelling with every mile. He found himself questioning what he was leaving behind and what lay ahead. The further he traveled, the faster his pulse raced, his anxiety mounting with each landmark slipping away in the rearview mirror.

The further Daniel drove, the more pronounced the whispers became. At first, he convinced himself it was just the wind weaving through the half-open window, but soon the noise intensified. It threaded itself between the rhythmic hum of the engine, the soft rustle of air outside, and even the music faintly playing from the radio. Every so often, Daniel could almost make out words, but they remained unintelligible, oddly urgent, and impossible to ignore.

Eventually, feeling overwhelmed and unsettled by the persistent whispers, Daniel stopped the car on a rural road. The fields stretched endlessly on either side, the stormy sky casting an eerie light on the quiet landscape. The only movement was a distant crow ascending into the air.

Daniel's hands gripped the steering wheel tightly as he shouted into the emptiness, desperate for answers.

"—RAT MS MT YEU —A0T 7FE1 1KO?"

He rested his forehead against the wheel, tears streaming down his face as he mumbled, "I can't keep listening to these incessant whispers; please, tell me what you want?"

The silence that followed was suffocating. The car hummed, the engine's sound filling the space as the wind rustled through the tall grasses outside. Sweat pooled in his palms as Daniel glanced nervously at the shadowy fields that stretched endlessly, the blades of grass trembling in the wind. His heartbeat thundered in his chest, matching the confusion and mounting fear swirling inside him.

Even as he pleaded into the void, the chill in the air seemed to thicken, and a sense of something watching—something unseen—grew stronger. The isolation of the moment intensified. Behind him, a crow called out, its voice amplifying his growing sense of vulnerability along the empty, desolate road.

For a moment, there was only the hum of the engine and the pounding of Daniel's heart. Then, without warning, he felt a cold breath on his neck, raising goosebumps along his skin. He froze.

A voice, clear and chilling, whispered in his ear: "You."

Daniel turned quickly, his heart pounding in his chest, only to find the back seat empty. A cold shiver ran down his spine as his breath hitched.

"Who's there? Show yourself!" Daniel demanded, his voice thick with tension.

The whisper answered, barely audible, a voice that seemed to emanate from everywhere and nowhere at once. "All we want is you, Daniel."

The words echoed in his ears, stirring up a fresh wave of dread. Panic briefly flickered in Daniel's mind, but he quickly suppressed it, grabbing the steering wheel with one hand and adjusting the gear stick with the other. He drove off, determined to push the encounter from his thoughts, but the oppressive atmosphere clung to him.

Daniel believed that by ignoring the whispers and the voice, he could negate their significance, but the persistent unease gnawed at him. No matter how hard he tried to focus on the road, his mind was overwhelmed with intrusive thoughts, spiraling anxiously between recent events—the whispers, the figures, Father Roberts' disbelief, and the growing fear that he had lost his mind entirely.

His knuckles turned white as he tightened his grip on the steering wheel, his jaw set in determination. He mentally replayed the events over and over—each whisper, each fleeting vision, the impossibility of it all.

Hours passed, the landscape blurring around him as he drove. Without realising how far he had gone, he had outpaced the city lights, the hum of traffic fading into the distance, until the roads gave way to the sweeping hills of Scotland. The rugged highlands unfolded before him, their towering silhouettes brooding under the heavy clouds.

Eventually, Daniel arrived at a remote hotel nestled in a secluded corner of the Scottish countryside. The building was an old stone construction, with parts of the exterior draped in moss, its traditional slate roof weathered by time. Standing two stories tall, the hotel appeared picturesque against the backdrop of the majestic mountains. The scent of damp earth mixed with the fresh, crisp air of the highlands, while the uneven stones of the pathway crunched under his feet. Ivy clung to the weathered walls, and a warm golden light spilled from the small windows, inviting him inside.

The entrance was marked by antique lanterns, their soft glow illuminating a rustic wooden door carved with intricate Celtic patterns. The hotel seemed like an oasis of timelessness, offering a tranquil retreat in the midst of the dramatic and untamed landscape.

The lobby was dimly lit, the air filled with the scent of aged timber and a distant trace of peat smoke. A small hearth fire crackled, its glow dancing over worn armchairs and faded tartan rugs. The soft flickering of the flames created a sense of warmth, yet something in the air felt off.

An elderly woman, slightly stooped but keen-eyed, welcomed him with a polite nod, her voice thick with a soft accent. Her hands rested lightly atop the reception desk, and her gaze seemed to linger on Daniel a little too long.

Outside, the mist had begun to roll in, swallowing the outlines of trees and hedges as the sky darkened. The sound of fresh rain drummed steadily against the window panes, adding to the sense of isolation. There was something strangely comforting about the solitude, but it was also unnerving, as if the landscape itself was closing in on him.

Two days later, the maid entered the room to change the towels and bedding. She immediately noticed the eerie silence and the sudden chill in the air. The curtains had been drawn tightly shut, casting deep shadows across the room.

The authorities were called shortly after. They discovered Daniel's body, his face frozen in a look of exhaustion and terror, an expression not often seen in someone so young—only thirty-four years old. There were no signs of prior heart conditions. The cause of death was determined to be heart failure, but there was something more that couldn't be explained.

The room, despite being undisturbed in most ways, felt suffocating with a heavy, stale air. The walls, ceiling, and even parts of the wooden furniture were covered in jagged, frantic etchings. Latin phrases had been scratched into every available surface—painfully etched with broken fingernails and, later, with keys when his hands could no longer manage the task. The walls seemed to bleed with the desperation of the effort. Traces of dried blood were visible beneath the jagged inscriptions.

Some phrases repeated endlessly: "Nuid est veritas" and "memento mori" looped around the doorframes and radiator. Faint traces of dried blood marked the grooves beneath splintered fingernails, hinting at frantic hours spent carving the words. The eerie silence that filled the room lingered long after the investigators had departed.

The last phrase, carved into the wall above the bed, was:

"Missa est. The mass is ended."

Whether you are attending church to pray or reflect on your life, visiting the library and finding solace among the quiet shelves, or simply at home alone surrounded by your thoughts, there is a gentle hush that fills the air if you listen attentively. You may notice subtle whispers, so faint they almost blend into silence. In this instance, these whispers are not prayers for Daniel, but rather, intended for you.

Chapter 7
The Desire Trap

Paul Veness, thirty-three years old, single, and unable to hold down a job for long, always viewed life as a game of patience and chance. His motto, "If you want it, just take it," wasn't about recklessness, but about a calculated understanding of the world's vulnerabilities. For Paul, every unlocked door, every unattended window was a potential score—nothing more, nothing less. His reputation as a career housebreaker was built on a pattern of meticulous planning and an uncanny ability to disappear just before the police could catch him. Yet beneath his hardened exterior lurked a mind that thrived on the thrill of the gamble and the quiet satisfaction of outsmarting the system.

On this particular afternoon, the pub's relaxed atmosphere and the clink of glasses were familiar comforts. Paul's sharp hearing caught snippets of a conversation— a couple discussing a weekend away at her father's house. The woman's assurance that their cat would be "completely safe" while they were away piqued his interest. Paul barely concealed his smirk. People who believed their homes were safe were the easiest marks.

The couple stood up to leave, their movements a synchronised dance of familiarity. The man, tall and slim with a neatly trimmed beard and glasses, gently helped the woman, who wore black slacks and an orange polo shirt, with her leather jacket. They exchanged a few words, smiling at each other, before heading towards the exit. Paul swallowed the last of his lager, glanced at the clock above the bar, and then waited a few minutes before discreetly following them home.

They resided in a modern twelve-storey apartment building with a sleek, tinted glass façade that allowed Paul to see which floor they lived on and the flat number. It had a private entrance with an elegantly decorated lobby, complete with plush seating. Visitors had to ring the specific apartment they wished to access using a shiny, stainless-steel intercom system mounted next to the entrance doors, and above them, a security camera watched.

Over the next few days, Paul monitored the apartment, noting the occupants' vehicle. On Friday, he watched them load the car with suitcases before departing.

On Saturday evening, Paul donned his black hoodie, cargo trousers, and black trainers. He approached the block of flats under the cover of darkness. The street was quiet, illuminated by dim streetlights that cast long shadows across the pavement. A light drizzle had begun, making the ground slick and adding a faint patter to the night's sounds.

Paul waited for someone to enter the block of flats so he could discreetly follow them inside, as attempting to manipulate the entrance system would be captured by the camera above the door. The cool night air carried the distant hum of traffic and the occasional rustling of leaves. Paul's breath formed small clouds in the chilly air as he scanned the surroundings for any signs of activity. His eyes, sharp and alert, fixed on the doorway, noting every flicker of movement. He checked his watch— the minute hand was ticking closer to his planned entry time. As he leaned against a nearby wall, blending into the darkened alleyway, Paul could feel the tension in his muscles. His heart pounded slowly, each beat echoing in his ears.

Finally, footsteps echoed along the damp pavement. A resident approached, their key fob glinting briefly in the soft light before they swiped it across the reader. The door buzzed, and the person pulled it open, stepping through unaware of the shadow trailing just behind. Paul slipped in silently, the door closing with a soft thud behind him. Inside, the lobby smelled of cleaning supplies. Paul moved swiftly but cautiously, aware that this was only the beginning of his night's task.

Inside, he navigated the stairwell and hallway quickly but quietly. As he stood outside the door, he took a deep breath, listened for a moment, and then went to work picking the lock. The click of the mechanism was almost inaudible, but it signified Paul's entry.

The apartment was neat and well-kept, suggesting the residents took pride in their home. Paul quickly scanned the room for valuables. He began with the lounge, where an expensive television and various electronics caught his eye, but he was after the smaller stuff. Methodically, he moved to the bedroom, opening drawers, wardrobes, and bedside cabinets, finding jewellery boxes and cash stashed away. As he worked, Paul maintained an alert presence, listening for any sounds.

Paul was about to enter the next room when he heard the voices of a couple arguing. Their argument escalated until they were outside the front, just about to enter their apartment. The woman's voice was shrill, angry, while the man's tone grew increasingly defensive. Paul quickly assessed his surroundings for an escape route. However, the only option was through the lounge and over the balcony.

The lounge was dimly lit, with a double sofa and a large coffee table blocking his path. He manoeuvred around it swiftly, trying to remain silent. Once on the balcony, Paul attempted to climb down by gripping the damp metal railings. The cold metal felt slick under his fingers, causing his heart to race. He took a deep breath and tried to steady himself. Unfortunately, he slipped, lost his grip, and fell four storeys. His body hurtled through the air before he landed on his back on a grass bank.

Paul awoke in an unfamiliar room. Someone had dressed him in a pair of silk blue pyjamas. To his surprise, he experienced no pain—instead, he felt remarkably well. He sat up slowly, carefully surveying his surroundings. The room didn't resemble a hospital; rather, it exuded a cosy and warm ambiance. The lighting was bright, and the bed was exceptionally large and comfortable. The bedside cabinet held a glass, a jug of water, and a packet of his favourite cigars. The walls were adorned with exquisite paintings, depicting serene landscapes and vibrant abstract art. A sizeable wardrobe stood next to a door, crafted from polished oak and engraved with intricate designs.

One wall comprised an entire window that offered a panoramic view of a sprawling city. The cityscape was bustling with life—cars whizzed by on the streets, and people hurried along the pavements. Tall skyscrapers reached toward the clouds, their glass surfaces reflecting the sunlight. Below, parks and gardens provided lush patches of greenery amidst the urban jungle. Paul could see a river winding its way through the city, glistening under the sun's rays. As he took all this in, he wondered where he was and how he had come to be in such a remarkable place.

He pulled the bedding back, swung his legs over the side of the bed, and was about to stand up when the door opened. A woman entered, appearing to be around six feet tall, dark-skinned, with long black hair cascading down her back and over her shoulders, wearing a pale green dress that shimmered in the light. Her eyes sparkled as she smiled warmly at Paul, revealing a set of perfectly aligned teeth. The room was filled with a faint scent of jasmine, adding to the surreal atmosphere.

"Good to see you awake, Paul. My name is Ashita, and I will be your guide. How are you feeling after your rest?" Ashita inquired as she closed the door and approached Paul.

"What do you mean by 'guide'?" Paul asked, his expression reflecting confusion.

"Please return to bed, and I will explain everything to you," Ashita said, standing at the foot of the bed as she waited for Paul to make himself comfortable.

"All right, please explain where I am and what you mean by being my guide," Paul demanded while pouring himself a glass of water from the jug.

"Very well, listen carefully, and should you need further

clarification, please ask. The other evening, you attempted to gain unauthorised access to Mr. and Mrs. Wander's apartment. However, they returned home earlier than expected due to an altercation between her husband and her father, which led them to cut their weekend short. In an attempt to escape, you tried to climb over the balcony, but unfortunately, you slipped and met your demise." Ashita responded. Before she could continue, Paul interrupted her.

"Wait, what? You're suggesting that I'm deceased? Dead? Game over? This must be some sort of joke. Who is responsible for this load of crap?" Paul stuttered, appearing frightened and bewildered, his mind racing to determine who might have orchestrated such a scenario.

"I understand what is happening here," Paul remarked with a laugh. "This is a setup. Behind that door, there must be a group of coppers waiting for me to confess. You can all come in now, lads, your little game's up!" Paul continued, folding his arms and laughing, anticipating the door to burst open.

"You have misunderstood the situation. You are dead. You ceased to be. It's the end of the road, and I'm here to guide you through this transition. Rest assured, there are no police officers behind that door. If you look beside your bed, you'll see a serving hatch. Please tell me your preferences for food and drink, and I will ensure you receive whatever you desire," Ashita replied, hoping Paul would believe her and accept that he had passed over.

"No, I'm dead and this..." Paul's mind seemed to drift as he surveyed the room—a comforting space with a view that any living person would love to have. "This is my new existence? A confined space that will provide sustenance, and you, a guide, to assist me in adjusting. I would like a substantial steak meal with all appropriate accompaniments, a large ice cream sundae, and a double whiskey," Paul stated with a subtle smile, hinting at acceptance mingled with curiosity.

Ashita smiled and walked over to the serving hatch. With a gentle touch, she activated it, causing a compartment to slide open smoothly. She produced all of Paul's requested items. There was a large steak, perfectly seared with grill marks, accompanied by golden fries and a fresh, crisp salad drizzled with a light vinaigrette. The ice cream sundae featured five distinct flavours—vanilla, chocolate, strawberry, mint, and salted caramel—all generously topped with bright red cherries and luscious strawberries cascading down the sides. The aroma of the steak permeated the room, mingling with the sweetness of the dessert, creating an enticing fragrance that made Paul's senses tingle with anticipation.

Paul looked at the food. He noticed it was served quickly, and it appeared appetising with a pleasant aroma. He then turned to Ashita. "Would you taste some of this for me, please?" Paul asked, offering his plate to Ashita.

"Why would you want me to taste your food? I no longer eat food. I've been here so long that my body does not crave it anymore. And remember, you're dead, so we cannot poison you," replied Ashita firmly.

"Sorry, I'm still adjusting to being dead. How come it was served so quickly?" asked Paul as he cut into his steak.

"You're no longer alive, and here, well, we do things differently. Whatever you need is provided instantly," replied Ashita, smiling at Paul. "Now eat and enjoy your meal. I'll be back shortly. By the way, are you satisfied with the scenery, or would you prefer something else?" She asked, pointing to the window.

"Are you suggesting that the city I see is actually an illusion?" Paul asked, intrigued. "Fascinating. I would greatly appreciate a view of a warm golden beach, complete with palm trees, a clear blue sky, and yachts sailing on the sea," Paul stated as he took another bite of his meal.

Almost instantly, the scene outside the window transformed to match his request. The once bustling cityscape slowly faded away, revealing a serene beach with golden sand that glittered under the bright sun. Tall palm trees swayed in the warm breeze, their fronds rustling softly. The sky turned a vibrant shade of blue, unmarred by clouds, creating a perfect backdrop for the white sails of yachts gliding gracefully across the sparkling sea. Seagulls could be heard calling in the distance as they dipped and soared above the water. Paul smiled contentedly, momentarily lost in the beauty of the newly appeared paradise.

"I am thoroughly enjoying this location. It is truly a representation of peak happiness," Paul stated, gazing out of the window with a sense of tranquillity. "This is exceptional," he continued.

"I will leave you now to enjoy your meal. Upon my return, I will provide you with a tour," Ashita responded as she exited the room.

After an hour, Ashita returned to Paul's room. He had finished his meal and was standing by an open window, observing the scenic view before him. The gentle sea breeze rustled the curtains, and the aroma of saltwater filled the air. Ashita approached the window and stood beside him; her presence seemed to add warmth to the serene scene.

"Are you prepared for a tour?" Ashita asked. "Your clothes are in the wardrobe. If there is anything you don't prefer, close the door, think of something you'd like to wear, and when you open it, it will be there for you." She gazed at the picturesque view of the beach and the setting sun, the sky painted in hues of orange and pink, casting a golden glow over the waves that lazily lapped at the shore.

Paul turned to her with a mix of curiosity and excitement, ready to explore the surroundings. He walked over to the wardrobe and meticulously examined the clothing, appreciating the design and colours—clothes he would have admired in his lifetime. He then paused to reflect, attempting to comprehend the situation, though it eluded his understanding.

"I don't understand all this," Paul said, holding a designer shirt in one hand and the wardrobe door in the other, looking more confused than ever. "The things I've eaten, the things I've seen—they're exactly what I've always wanted. The room is exactly how I would have liked it, these clothes are the ones I would have chosen when I was alive, and you... well, you match my ideal woman."

Paul's eyes scanned the pristine room from corner to corner. The plush carpet felt so soft under his feet, reminiscent of the one he had always wanted in his bedroom but could never afford. The walls were adorned with artwork that mirrored his tastes perfectly, each piece evoking memories of galleries he'd once visited. He walked to a small table by the window, where a steaming cup of his favourite exotic tea awaited him, its aroma filling the air with a comforting scent.

Even the temperature of the room was just right—neither too warm nor too cold. As he stood there in bewilderment, he couldn't help but marvel at the uncanny precision with which every detail aligned with his preferences.

And then there was Ashita, the woman standing opposite him, whose every feature and gesture seemed to be drawn directly from his dreams. Her smile, her voice, even the way she looked at him—all of it matched the image he had conjured in his mind. Paul's confusion grew deeper, yet he felt an inexplicable sense of belonging in this perfect replication of his desires.

Paul's brow furrowed as he looked over at Ashita. He had known longing—a hunger for connection, for fulfilment—but now, in this surreal space, everything felt both too perfect and utterly disorienting.

"Ashita," he finally managed, his voice trembling, "what is this place? Who are you really? And why am I here?"

Ashita's eyes softened, a gentle smile touching her lips. She moved closer, her presence both calming and unsettling.

"Paul," she said softly, "this is a realm beyond your previous understanding. It's a place where your deepest desires are realised—without the pain, the disappointment, the limitations of your former life."

He took a hesitant step back. "But… why me? Why am I here? What do you want from me?"

She reached out, her hand hovering just above his.

"Because you've been searching for something—something that seemed just out of reach. I am here to help you fulfil your every desire. Think of me as a mirror of what you truly crave. I am the embodiment of your ideal, your perfect woman—what you wanted, what you need, all in one."

Paul's eyes darted to her, suspicion flickering beneath his confusion. "And what's the catch? Nothing in life—sorry, in death—is that simple."

Ashita chuckled softly, a sound like tinkling bells. "There's no catch. Only understanding. You've carried burdens, regrets, and unmet hopes. Here, those are dissolved. You can have everything—love, companionship, fulfilment—without the scars of the past."

He hesitated, feeling both tempted and wary of this seemingly perfect place. "It seems almost too good to be true. How can I ensure that this is not some form of deception?"

She maintained her composed demeanour. "How could something so beautiful be misleading? Whatever you are seeking, you will find it here, in this realm."

Paul's thoughts were filled with inquiries about the nature of this realm, Ashita's true identity, and what lay beyond the bedroom door. The allure of promised fulfilment was strong, yet a hint of scepticism remained.

"Is this reality, or am I in a state of unconsciousness?" he asked quietly, gazing out of the window.

Ashita replied with a gentle smile, her eyes exuding both warmth and enigma. "It is real enough for your needs. Embrace your desires."

"I will leave you to change," Ashita remarked, touching his arm gently before exiting the room. Paul felt a shiver from her touch as he proceeded to open the wardrobe. Inside, he found a selection of finely tailored clothes. He changed into a red silk shirt that shimmered under the light, black trousers that fit him perfectly, and a pair of polished black shoes.

He then sat on the foot of the bed and contemplated his desire for four thousand pounds. The room was quiet except for the sound of crashing waves and the seagulls coming in from the window. Rising slowly from the bed, he felt a hint of anticipation as he approached the hatch. He slid it open cautiously. To his astonishment, there lay four thousand pounds in crisp, new notes, neatly stacked. The notes had a faint smell of ink and paper, indicating their freshness. He found it challenging to believe what he saw, wondering if it was some kind of trick or if this realm truly did give you what you desired.

As Paul stood at the hatch, running his hands over the money, Ashita re-entered the room, adorned in a patterned red saree that glimmered in the sunlight streaming through the window.

"I see you have discovered how to utilise the hatch for purposes beyond food and drink," Ashita remarked with a sly smile, closing the door softly behind her and approaching Paul, her bangles jingling with each step.

Paul looked at Ashita, his eyes wide with admiration. "You look remarkable," he said, taking in the intricate details of her attire and the grace with which she carried herself.

Ashita's eyes sparkled with amusement. "Thank you. I only wear this saree on special occasions."

Paul nodded, still captivated by her appearance. "It suits you perfectly."

With a gentle laugh, Ashita gestured towards the door. "Come, I will provide a tour of this extraordinary realm. There is much for you to see and experience. Remember, you may request anything you desire, and it will be provided." Her voice was filled with promise and mystery.

Ashita led Paul through streets lined with shops offering a variety of goods. The aroma from some stores was intense, reminiscent of scents he recalled from his childhood. As they continued, he marvelled at the vibrant displays in each window, showcasing everything from fresh produce to handcrafted trinkets. The lively chatter of shopkeepers and customers filled the air, creating a symphony of voices that added to the bustling atmosphere. Paul paused to admire a stall selling vividly coloured fabrics, their patterns evoking memories of family gatherings where such textiles adorned the tables. He wondered about the absence of his parents or grandparents, finding it unusual that he had not encountered any family members who had passed away.

Paul grasped Ashita's hand and pulled her aside. "Why have I not seen any of my family members who have passed away? Where are they?" He asked, his voice tinged with confusion and desperation.

Ashita looked into Paul's eyes with a calm yet solemn expression. "Your family is not here. You will never see them again," she explained softly. "What you see here is solely for you. This is all created for you alone."

Paul looked around at his surroundings, trying to comprehend this unfamiliar realm—the shops, the smells—everything brought back memories from his childhood. He had never felt so alone.

"Look, I do not belong here. Heaven is not for me. My place is in Hell. I am sorry," Paul asserted, his voice trembling with conviction. He felt a deep-seated guilt gnawing at him, memories of past deeds flashing before his eyes.

Ashita gently placed a hand on his shoulder, her touch warm and reassuring. "Paul, this is not Heaven. This is Hell, and here you will stay."

Paul stood there, unable to believe he was in Hell. The air started to grow thick and oppressive, with a faint smell of sulphur lingering. He looked around as the shops began to melt away, replaced by a bleak, dreary landscape filled with twisted, demonic figures lurking in every shadow. Panic surged through his veins, and he ran as fast as he could.

He stumbled into a dark alley, and at the bottom of it, he could see a shop, its neon lights spelling out "WELCOME." Paul ran towards the shop and stumbled through its doors. Inside, he could see ghostly images of his family members pointing at him and laughing. Then, without warning, he found himself back in his bedroom, lying in bed just as he had been when he first woke up. The transition was seamless, making him question what was real. Everything appeared the same—the view from his window showed the city again, bustling with life.

At that moment, the door opened, and Ashita walked in.

"You cannot escape. This is your home now. Throughout your life, you desired everything, and now it is all yours," she said with a cryptic smile. Her eyes glowed with an unnatural light, contrasting with her otherwise human appearance. "Every game you play, you will win. Everything you desire is yours, and if you get bored, we start from the beginning."

Ashita's voice was soothing yet unsettling, like a serpent

whispering promises of endless pleasure. She walked gracefully toward Paul, bringing him a tray with steak and an ice cream sundae. The aroma of the perfectly cooked steak, mixed with the sweetness of the sundae, reminded Paul of his happiest moments. Yet, there was an underlying dread, knowing the food was part of his endless torment.

There are times when people desire things they do not have. Some individuals spend their lives working to achieve these desires that they may never attain, and some may even break the law to accomplish them. However, it is worth considering whether this pursuit is truly valuable. It may be beneficial to appreciate what one already has. For instance, Paul discovered that achieving everything he wanted seemed like a dream come true, but whether this leads to true happiness is up for debate. It is important to consider the potential consequences of one's wishes and desires.

Chapter 8
Honeywicke

Honeywicke Village, England, 1710

On a July afternoon, villagers gathered in the square as storm clouds gathered overhead. There had been no rain for several weeks, and there seemed to be no end to the drought. Smoke filled the air as more people gathered to watch a witch being burned. In the centre of the cobbled square, a pyre made of alder branches and elm logs had been assembled.

The oppressive heat clung to the ground, and even the possibility of rain lingered above. Many townsfolk wiped beads of sweat from their brows while waiting anxiously. Women fanned themselves with their hands, children tugged at sleeves and whispered questions, and men shifted uneasily, glancing at the brewing clouds.

The crowd watched the growing structure at the centre of the square, its rough wood tacked together with care and purpose by several strong men earlier in the day. The smells of burning torches and sweat mingled in the air as children stood close to their mothers, and elders discussed the trial in low voices, exchanging serious looks and murmured words about justice and tradition.

Houses surrounding the square had darkened windows, with shutters moving in the increasing wind. Some faces peered cautiously through the cracks in the shutters, unwilling to join but unable to look away. The gathering aimed to address recent difficulties, including poor crop yields, livestock deaths, and the ongoing drought—hardships that had gripped the village with fear and suspicion.

Dary Mletcher, who lived alone on the village outskirts, was accused by the community of causing these problems through alleged witchcraft. Her trial lasted less than twenty minutes before she was found guilty, with villagers packed tightly together, listening to accusations and all the evidence that had been gathered.

The verdict brought a tense silence, broken only by the distant rumble of thunder and the shuffling of feet as preparations for punishment began.

Tied to the stake, Dary Mletcher didn't scream. The mob did that for her.

"Burn the witch!"

"She cursed my son!"

"My herd of cows died when she walked past them!"

"You're the Devil's whore!"

Dary directed her attention beyond the shouting mob, her dark eyes settling on the solitary figure who remained silent. Judge Thomas Stranger stood apart, identifiable by his tall, thin stature and pale complexion, dressed formally in a powdered wig and black coat, his lips set in a firm line. He held a torch in his right hand.

The flickering light of the torch cast shifting shadows across the judge's austere face, accentuating the deep lines of concentration etched around his mouth. Though voices and laughter swelled behind her, Dary could make out the faint tremor in Stranger's grip, hinting at a tension beneath his composed exterior. The scent of dry wood mingled with the faint aroma of burning oil as wisps of smoke curled upward. Despite the commotion, an air of solemnity seemed to radiate from the judge, setting him further apart from those around him.

"Say your final words," shouted the judge.

Dary gave a piercing, haunting smile, her gaze locking with his.

"You will die, Stranger," she said, loud enough for every man, woman, and child to hear. "Not today. But the day you reach forty, you will die. And so will your sons. And so will their sons. When the thirty-fifth Stranger male first bleeds, I shall return. I will tear the marrow from your line. Then you will light this pyre—and I shall burn your name to cinders."

Thomas paused for a moment, his breath quickening as he studied the restless crowd gathered in a wide circle around the makeshift pyre. He stepped forward slowly, his boots crunching on the cobblestones. With trembling hands, he met Dary's gaze—her eyes steady and unblinking despite the tension in the air. The flickering torch cast harsh shadows across her face as Thomas lowered it to the pile of branches and twigs at her feet, setting them alight. The flames crackled and climbed, casting an orange glow that danced over the anxious faces in the crowd.

Dary did not scream, but she did laugh.

Honeywicke, England—Present Day

Edward Stranger is a teacher, devoted husband to Sam, and attentive father to their four-year-old son, Michael. Passionate about teaching, Edward is known for his patience and curiosity, always encouraging his students and loved ones to ask questions and seek understanding. His relationship with Sam is one of mutual respect and affection, built over years of shared experiences and challenges. With Michael, Edward enjoys passing down family stories, reading together at bedtime, and exploring parks during weekends.

Edward's mother had explained to him that the family home in Honeywicke is scheduled to be sold in several months, requesting that he assess and potentially sell some of the furniture while ensuring it remains in good condition.

The Honeywicke house, a picture of the Stranger lineage for generations, holds countless memories—childhood visits, Christmas gatherings, and family funerals. Many of the furnishings have been in the family for decades, each piece carrying its own bit of history. Throughout Edward's upbringing, his mother discussed the family curse; however, Edward regarded such beliefs as fictional tales intended to entertain or frighten children. His mother spoke of lost fortunes, mysterious illnesses, and untimely deaths among the male side of the family, all occurring at the age of forty.

However, Edward maintained that his father's death at work, occurring at the age of forty, was purely accidental, dismissing any suggestions of supernatural influence or curse. For him, the idea of a curse is rooted in myth rather than reality—a story passed along but never truly believed. Despite his scepticism, a sense of unease lingers each time he returns to Honeywicke.

As Edward crossed the threshold of Honeywicke, a thousand memories seemed to press against his mind, each one whispering from the shadowed corners and sunlit alcoves. The house greeted him with its familiar hush, the air thick with dust and the faint aroma of old violets, a scent he remembered from his grandmother's linen chests. Every step he took stirred the silence—floorboards creaked, and his footsteps echoed through the high-ceilinged hallway like hesitant questions.

He moved deliberately, passing through rooms layered with the remnants of family life. The parlour was just as he remembered—the grand piano, its mahogany body dulled with age, rested against the far wall, its lid shut as though still in mourning. Edward paused, trailing his fingers over the piano's surface, tracing the pattern of dust that time had left behind. On the mantelpiece, tarnished silver and gold frames displayed the faces of ancestors—stern men in tailcoats and women in stiff dresses, all staring out as if to remind him of the family's long, troubled legacy.

He took out his notebook, listing each item he might need to assess—the sturdy oak armoire in the upstairs hallway, its doors swollen with age; the battered wingback chairs by the mullioned window, their faded upholstery marked by generations; and the dining table, its surface gouged from decades of games, feasts, and whispered secrets. He ran his hand over the banisters, feeling the worn places where children's hands had slid on their way down for breakfast and where adults had gripped tightly during moments of sorrow.

Sam carried the overnight bags inside and paused briefly to admire the impressive features of the house, wishing momentarily that they could move in and make it their home. She loved the high ceiling in the hallway, how the sunlight poured in through the tall windows onto the polished wooden floors, and the intricate mouldings along the walls. Sam then set down the luggage and proceeded to fetch Michael and their dog Archie from the car.

As night settled over Honeywicke, the rain intensified, rattling against the ancient windows as if it were eager to get inside. The wind moaned along the eaves, twisting the silhouettes of garden trees into grotesque shapes upon the walls.

Upstairs, Michael slept fitfully, mumbling to himself, while Sam tried to distract herself with unpacking; her nerves were on edge for some reason, and she couldn't understand why.

Edward proceeded through the intricate corridors of the house, his footsteps echoing off the oak panels on the walls. Each creak and groan that issued from the aging structure seemed not merely coincidental but as though the house itself was drawing attention to its long history. The air was tinged with a faint mustiness, mingled with the scent of old paper and polished brass.

Edward entered the library; ancestral portraits occupied the shadowed walls, their painted eyes tracing every movement Edward made. Heavy velvet curtains muffled the rain rattling on the windows. The faces in the brass-coloured frames, rendered in sombre oils, appeared to scrutinise him with an intensity that bordered on accusation, their lips pursed and brows furrowed.

The largest portrait commanded the space above the ornate marble fireplace. It depicted Thomas Stranger, whose imposing presence was amplified by his tailored coat and unwavering gaze. Layers of dust had settled on the gilded frame, and the light coming from the hallway played strange tricks on the canvas, casting moving shadows that seemed almost alive. As Edward gazed at the painting, he felt a chill run down his spine— a sense of being watched and judged.

When Edward turned away, the sensation lingered, and catching the portrait from the corner of his eye, he noticed a subtle shift in Stranger's stern expression—a slight, knowing smirk seemed to have formed. Startled, Edward looked back directly, but the face had reverted to its original severity, leaving him uncertain whether the change had been real or imagined. The ambiguity unsettled him further, deepening the mysteries of the house and its silent observers.

As Edward turned to walk out of the library, he heard a whisper from a male voice.

"When the thirty-fifth Stranger male first bleeds, she will return, and Michael is the thirty-fifth male."

Edward turned around quickly, but there was no one else there; apart from him, the room was empty. "Who's there? Don't hide; show yourself." He listened for a moment and scanned the room for movement. Edward left the library, quickly closed the door, and made his way to the bedroom, back to Sam and Michael.

He hurried down the hallway, his heart hammering against his chest, his ears straining for any further traces of the voice. The storm's din had faded into a steady patter, but within Honeywicke, the silence had deepened, thick and uneasy. Edward's mind raced with the cryptic message: *Michael is the thirty-fifth*. What did it mean? Who was or is *"she"* who would return?

Sam looked up as Edward burst into the bedroom, her eyes wide and searching. Michael still tossed in uneasy sleep, his brow damp despite the chill. Edward hesitated, unsure whether to speak of what he had just heard, the old house's gloom pressing against him from every side. He chose silence instead, checking the locks on the windows and making sure the curtains were pulled tight.

Edward lingered by the door, listening to the ambient sounds within the old house; there was water dripping from an indeterminate source in the darkness. The faint echo of each droplet resonated against silent walls, blending with the distant creaks of the settling floorboards. He closed the door softly behind him, careful not to disturb the fragile quiet.

He approached Sam, who was standing by the window, looking into the garden and noting the movement of tree silhouettes against the night sky. The glass was cool beneath her fingertips as she traced the outline of a swaying branch, her breath briefly fogging the pane. Outside, moonlight occasionally broke through the drifting clouds, painting shifting patterns onto the grass.

Edward took Sam's hand, his grip gentle yet determined, acknowledging through this gesture their mutual understanding to comfort each other, whatever may come. Sam glanced at him, her eyes reflecting worry and resolve; together, they listened to the world outside while bracing themselves for what lay ahead. Sam still felt like something was about to happen; she had never felt this way before, and found the feeling unsettling.

Edward sat in an armchair by the fireplace, picked up his book, and turned on the lamp on a nearby table. Sam turned off the main light and settled next to Michael on the bed.

The faint glow coming from the fireplace illuminated Edward's face as he adjusted his reading glasses and settled deeper into the worn cushions, the crackling fire casting shifting shadows on the walls.

Archie, his loyal terrier, glanced up at Edward, yawned widely, revealing his tiny teeth, and then lay back down on his blanket, curling into a tight ball for warmth.

Outside, the storm increased in intensity; rain lashed against the windows, and the wind howled through the trees, occasionally rattling the windows. Thunder rumbled in the distance, and flashes of lightning briefly lit up the room, followed by a chorus of raindrops drumming on the windows. The atmosphere was thick with tension, yet inside, the air was heavy and still.

After about an hour and a half, Michael, who had been tossing restlessly in his sleep, suddenly woke up shouting and screaming, his voice echoing off the walls. Blood streamed from his nose, staining his upper lip and chin. Sam woke quickly, startled by his cries, her heart pounding in her chest as she sat up and tried to help Michael. Edward, momentarily shocked, responded by grabbing a clean towel from his bag to stop the bleeding, his hands steady but concern etched on his brow.

At that moment, the reading lamp flickered, its light unsteady as the power struggled against the storm. Within seconds, the lamp went out completely, plunging the house into darkness. Only the faint orange embers in the fireplace provided any light, casting dancing shadows on the worried faces gathered around Michael.

Suddenly, the fire roared, and then the front door burst open with a crash. Wind moved through the doorway and up the stairs, accompanied by laughter and a woman's voice shouting out,

"Michael is the thirty-fifth, and he has bled; I have returned."

The bedroom door opened abruptly; Edward and Sam, still

attending to Michael, looked up at the door. Edward felt his skin prickle with dread while Sam gripped Michael tightly, her breath caught in her throat. The room was thick with tension, and both Edward and Sam stared wide-eyed at the empty hallway beyond, struggling to process what they had just witnessed. Edward walked to the bedside table, picked up the candlestick, lit it, and held the candle in front of himself.

It was no longer a whisper in the library. It was here, in the air between him and the hallway. Then the smell came—acrid and heavy, like a bonfire drenched in tar. The candlelight trembled as a faint trail of smoke slithered into the bedroom and began spreading along the floor, winding its way towards Edward and Sam. Archie reacted to the smoke by barking and cautiously approaching before retreating from it.

Edward's heart hammered in his chest. "Who's there?" he called, his voice hoarse.

The smoke billowed and twisted, pooling thickly at the doorway before its edges tightened, limbs forming and shifting in the gloom. The cloying aroma hung heavy in the air, sharp and almost floral, mingling with an undercurrent of something rotten. As the smoke thinned, details sharpened. Dary Mletcher's outline grew clearer. She stepped forward, tendrils of lingering smoke still curling around her as if reluctant to let go. Her skin was blackened and cracked, glowing in places with veins of molten orange, as though embers still smoldered beneath her rotten flesh. Strands of burnt hair clung to her scalp, and her dress—or what was left of it—hung in charred tatters. The air shimmered with heat around her.

Edward stumbled back, knocking Sam onto the bed. His mouth was dry. "You're not real; you're part of my nightmare," he whispered.

Dary's lips cracked into a slow smile, ash drifting from them as she spoke. "You wear Thomas Stranger's face."

Edward shook his head violently. "I'm not him; whatever he did has nothing to do with me. I'm nothing like him!"

"You burn with his blood." Her voice was layered—one voice, then another beneath it, and then another, as if every person Thomas claimed before her spoke with her.

The heat in the room spiked. The candle's flame elongated, twisting towards her like it was bowing. Smoke began to fill the room and crawl up Edward's legs, wrapping around his waist and then around Sam, twisting and turning around their bodies.

They tried to run past her, but the doorway stretched like a mirage—no matter how many steps they took or how hard they tried, they were still in the same spot, the same suffocating heat pressing in from all sides.

Dary raised a hand, her fingers ending in jagged black nails, and touched Edward's cheek. The burn was instant, blistering his skin. He screamed, swatting her away, but she only tilted her head, studying him like a cat playing with her prey.

"I've waited many centuries to punish this," she breathed, the embers in her chest flaring. "Your life ends here with your whore; it ends in fire like mine did, and your son Michael will be mine."

The walls began to glow red, as though the house itself had caught alight from within. And then the rumble as the flames came.

The flames came fast, blooming from floorboards like molten flowers, racing along the walls in spirals that hissed and cracked as they devoured the timber. The heat was unbearable—the kind that stole breath before you could scream. Edward and Sam stumbled into the corner as the room twisted; smoke clawed its way down their throats, choking them. Somewhere in the haze, Dary's laughter rilled like hot oil.

"Feel my pain, feel your skin melt like mine." Her voice came from everywhere at once.

The fire surged, swallowing Edward and Sam in a roaring, blinding inferno. And then, silence.

When the flames vanished, there was nothing left in the room but scorched walls and a blackened floor... and two heaps of ashes where Edward and Sam had been.

Firefighters moved carefully through the ruins, boots crunching over brittle debris. The house had gone up fast, too hot for any cause—no faulty wiring, no lightning strike. The investigators would find nothing but a sudden, consuming blaze.

Fire Chief Jilkes wiped the sweat from his brow despite the

morning chill. *"We've searched every inch,"* he told the police inspector. *"There are no bodies."*

The inspector frowned. *"Are you sure? Their car is still here."*

"No bodies; we've searched everywhere," replied Jilkes as he walked away.

On a charred wall in the bedroom, someone—or something—had written with a finger dipped in soot:

The line burns still.

In a flat in Danchester, Dary Mletcher sat at her kitchen table feeding her four-year-old son, Michael, when news broke about a fire at a manor house in Honeywicke. Reports indicated that two adults and a child were still missing. The reporter's voice was tense. *"Fire crews are still searching the remains of Honeywicke Manor, where smoke still pours from the ruins."* The camera panned across the charred estate, emergency vehicles crowding the grand drive.

Dary began to laugh as she rose to give her dog, Archie, the portion of breakfast that Michael had not wanted.

Chapter 9
The Last Advice

Lenny Hyland is not a typical individual. He temporarily paused his life to care for his ill father, which also affected his romantic relationships. Now that his father has passed away, Lenny recognised that he needed to get his life back on track. After covering the funeral expenses, he found that his savings were limited. While he had saved some cash for bills, he recognised the necessity of securing employment. At twenty-six years old, he felt it was impractical to attend college and acquire new skills, so he considered work in bars or restaurants. Although there were job openings at the local fast-food restaurant, they did not appeal to him at this stage.

Lenny's decision to put his life on hold had emotional consequences as well. He felt a mix of sadness and relief after his father's passing, coupled with anxiety about rebuilding his life from scratch. He spent his days reflecting on his next steps. Determined to regain a sense of purpose, Lenny kept exploring opportunities that would allow him to rebuild his confidence and financial stability. He reached out to old friends, hoping their advice or connections might lead to suitable employment.

One afternoon, feeling dejected after another unsuccessful job interview—his fourth of the day—he questioned whether the catering industry was truly the right path for him as he made his way home. He felt a heaviness in his chest and an overwhelming sense of doubt about his future. The bustling city streets offered little comfort, with people hurrying past him, absorbed in their own lives.

As he turned the corner, he unexpectedly collided with an old friend from school. Lenny hadn't seen Fran in over five years. They had intended to stay in touch, but when Fran relocated to a city up north for work and Lenny's father fell seriously ill, their friendship was regrettably set aside. Fran looked different now, dressed sharply in a business suit, carrying a briefcase. Lenny couldn't help but feel a twinge of envy, wondering what career path Fran had taken.

"Fran?" Lenny stammered, surprised by the chance encounter.

"Well, well! How have you been?" Fran smiled warmly, though there was a hint of surprise in his eyes. "Lenny! Wow, this is unexpected. I've been good, just so busy with work. And you? How's everything on your end?"

The two men stood there discussing their recent activities and reminiscing about the past. When Lenny mentioned that he had attended his fourth interview of the day but wasn't having any success, Fran's expression shifted slightly.

"Please don't take this the wrong way, but Lenny, you shouldn't go to an interview in a jumper, jeans, and trainers. You need to get a suit or something smart. If you visit a charity shop, they might have some affordable suits," Fran advised, aiming to offer helpful suggestions without discouraging his friend. Fran remembered how he had struggled with job interviews himself and wanted to share what he had learned. Fran's eyes showed genuine concern as he spoke, hoping his advice would be taken positively. His words were gentle but firm, trying to steer Lenny in the right direction without sounding critical.

"Thanks for the advice, Fran. That just might help," Lenny replied, seeming to find renewed enthusiasm from Fran's guidance. Feeling optimistic about the future, he decided to dress more appropriately for his next interview, imagining himself in a smart suit making a strong impression.

Lenny had wanted to buy a suit, but after the funeral expenses and other bills, there was limited money available, so he had to make do with what he had. The costs had been overwhelming, from the coffin to the flowers, and left little room for additional purchases. However, Fran had given him some practical advice that might improve his situation. He suggested exploring charity shops as a viable option.

Lenny had never considered going into a charity shop. They always reminded him of the jumble sales he attended as a child, which often had an unusual smell, and most of the items were not of high quality. Those childhood memories were filled with dusty old toys and clothes piled high on makeshift tables, always smelling faintly of mildew and mothballs.

Fran assured him that modern charity shops were quite different, often carrying gently used, high-quality items donated by people who no longer needed them. Some even carried brand-name suits and accessories at a fraction of the retail price. With his new perspective, Lenny decided to give charity shops a try, hoping to find something suitable for his needs without further straining his finances.

The following morning, Lenny decided to visit several charity shops in town to find a suit or outfit suitable for a job interview. He didn't want to appear untidy at his next interview. He was willing to spend £24, or maybe he could stretch to £40. As he walked down the high street, he contemplated the style of suit he desired—perhaps something dark and classic, or maybe a bit more modern with sharp lines and a slimmer fit.

However, the first few charity shops he visited didn't have anything that fit him. One shop had an oversized blazer that looked like it belonged in the 1980s, while another had trousers that were too short. Despite these setbacks, the shopkeepers were friendly and encouraging, suggesting other stores he might try. While he found some items appealing, like a vintage leather jacket that was sadly out of his budget and a pair of stylish shoes that didn't match his needs, he remained determined to find a suit. He continued his search with determination, hoping that the next shop would hold the perfect outfit for his upcoming interview.

After visiting six charity shops without finding a suitable suit, Lenny considered purchasing a shirt, tie, and pair of trousers instead. This would require more searching through the charity shops, which he found unappealing. He felt frustrated and tired from the constant searching, wondering if he would ever find what he needed.

Upon entering the next charity shop, he noticed that it had a large selection of clothing, some of which appeared to be of good quality for second-hand items. The shop was brighter and better organised than the previous ones, making it easier to browse through the racks. He noted the variety of colours and fabrics, hoping to find something that would fit both his size and style preferences. As he scanned the rows of clothes, he felt a glimmer of hope that this shop might have just what he needed.

As he scanned the rows of jackets and suits, hoping to find something affordable, his eye was drawn to a particular suit. It stood out like a beacon of refinement amidst the ordinary, with its distinguished dark colour, style, and meticulous stitching. The fabric shimmered slightly under the fluorescent lights, revealing a fine weave that promised comfort and durability. The suit appeared almost out of place, yet there it hung, seemingly destined for him.

Without hesitation, he picked it up and checked the size—it was perfect. He could already imagine not only wearing it to the job interview but to important meetings or even some kind of special event, exuding confidence and elegance. However, there was no price tag. He brought it to the counter and inquired about the price from the elderly lady who had a warm smile and kind eyes behind her glasses.

"That's just come in," said the elderly lady, taking the suit from Lenny and placing it on the counter with care. Her movements were slow but precise, indicating years of experience and respect for quality garments.

"How much is it?" Lenny asked as he took out his wallet, trying to hide his excitement.

"We typically sell suits for about £19, but I will verify the price for you," replied the elderly lady. With that, she walked to the back of the shop and through a door marked *Staff Only*.

While waiting for her return, Lenny could hardly believe his luck—finding a beautiful suit in his size at such a reasonable price. He envisioned himself turning heads and receiving compliments for his impeccable taste. The lady returned with a small notebook in her hand and informed Lenny that the suit was priced at £14, as it was a medium size. She smiled warmly as she spoke, making Lenny feel even more thrilled with his purchase. He also purchased two white shirts, three ties, and a pair of shoes, nearly all within his budget. While walking home, he passed a dry cleaner and considered how much better the suit would look if it was pressed and cleaned properly.

The suit had seen days of grandeur, but time had dulled its charm. The idea of freshening up the suit and bringing it to its former glory brought a smile to his face.

He entered the dry cleaner, a small shop with old-fashioned décor and a faint chemical scent lingering in the air. He handed his suit to the man behind the counter, a man whose broad Scottish accent immediately set him apart. The man carefully examined the suit, noted the slight discolouration, then wrote out a ticket and tore it in half. He handed one half to Lenny.

"It'll be ready on Tuesday. You'll need to pay now," said the man, his tone both friendly and businesslike.

"Yes, that's fine. How much will it be?" asked Lenny, hoping he had sufficient funds. He fumbled in his pocket looking for his wallet. When he opened it, he saw the two twenty-pound notes, the last of his money until next week.

"That'll be £22.70, please," replied the man, ringing it up in the till with practiced motion.

Lenny glanced at the amount displayed on the till and felt relieved. He was pleased that he still had some money left over, albeit not much, but enough for the next few days. He handed over the cash, thanked the man, and stepped back onto the street, feeling a little happier. Knowing that his suit would be ready on Tuesday and his job interview was on Wednesday afternoon made him feel optimistic about his future.

The weekend passed quickly, and before Lenny realised, it was already Tuesday. He went to retrieve his suit from the dry cleaner and then hurried home to see how he would look in the suit, with the new shoes, shirt, and tie. Upon donning the suit, Lenny found that it fit him perfectly, as if tailored specifically for his frame. The jacket hugged his shoulders and torso just right, while the trousers fell in a sharp, clean line down to his newly polished shoes. The fabric felt smooth against his skin, imparting a surge of confidence unlike anything he had previously experienced. The fine stitching and craftsmanship were apparent, giving the suit exquisite quality.

He stood taller, his gestures became more refined, and his walk exuded effortless grace. His previously casual demeanour was replaced by a sense of sophistication. When he glanced at himself in the mirror, he noticed a glimmer in his eyes and a proud tilt of his chin. It appeared that the suit possessed an energy and presence that seemed to permeate his very being. With each movement, the suit seemed to amplify his self-assurance, transforming not just his appearance, but his entire attitude.

On the morning of the job interview, Lenny woke up early to prepare himself. Feeling nervous, he decided to skip breakfast and opt for a mug of tea instead. He sat at the kitchen table, looking out of the window at the few grey clouds drifting by, while listening to the birds chirping. His thoughts wandered to his suit and how it made him feel. It was unusual; he had never experienced clothing bestowing such confidence before. The suit seemed to give him self-belief, as though he could overcome any challenge life threw at him.

He spent the rest of the morning ironing his shirt meticulously, smoothing out every crease until it was flawless. Then, he showered, letting the warm water relax him, and shaved carefully to avoid any nicks. Finally, he dressed methodically, adjusting his tie so it sat perfectly. Glancing in the mirror, he took a deep breath, and a surge of determination seemed to run through him. He collected his documents and house keys, had one last look at himself in the mirror, and then left the house.

Lenny entered the hotel and proceeded to the reception. The hotel had an old-style ambience, with a grand staircase and oak-panelled walls adorned with paintings of woodland scenes. He approached the reception desk confidently, which was unusual for him, as he typically felt anxious, fiddling with his keys or loose change in his pockets. He waited patiently for the young female receptionist to finish her telephone conversation.

"Good afternoon, I am here to see Sophie Quintle," Lenny inquired, smiling politely at the receptionist.

The woman returned his smile, entered some information into her computer, and made a note in her notebook.

"If you take the lift to the second floor, turn right, and proceed to the third door along on the left, Sophie will be waiting for you, Mr. Hyland," she said.

Normally, by now, he would be panicking, but walking along the hallway, he felt calm. The hallway was decorated with paintings depicting the changing seasons, adding to his sense of tranquillity. He reached the door and knocked loudly. The sound echoed in the quiet hallway.

The door was opened by a woman who appeared to be around sixty years old and stood about five feet tall. She wore a long grey skirt and a cream-coloured blouse, her silver hair neatly trimmed into a bob. "Good afternoon, Mr. Hyland, please come in and take a seat," said Sophie. Her voice was warm and welcoming.

Lenny took a seat facing a large wooden desk with numerous folders meticulously organised and two photos of some children, one of whom seemed to be holding a kite and the other smiling at a birthday party.

Sophie took her seat, made herself comfortable, and began the interview. The room was filled with sunlight streaming through a large window, illuminating the polished surface of the desk. The questions came, and Lenny answered them clearly and confidently. His expressions were varied, his tone engaging. Sophie followed this display of character with interest, occasionally nodding and jotting down notes in her leather-bound notebook.

It was only after Lenny had left the interview that he noticed something unusual. During the interview, he experienced an inexplicable compulsion, guiding his mannerisms and behaviours in unexpected ways. His speech adopted an unintended rhythm, and his gestures, he then realised—it was the suit. It somehow provided him with confidence, pulling him out of his shell and instructing him on what to do and how to do it.

Lenny needed to know the origin of the suit and its previous owner. He promptly went to the charity shop to inquire about the donor of the suit. However, upon arrival, he found that the charity shop was gone— abandoned. There was dirt and grime all over the windows, and there were a few 'Help Wanted' posters that had been there for a long time, judging by the dates on them. A large chain was wrapped around the door handles, covered with dust and cobwebs, suggesting that the shop had been unoccupied for years.

Feeling perplexed, Lenny looked around to verify he was at the correct location. The street was busy with shoppers and road traffic. He identified the neighbouring pizza parlour from his previous visit. The smell of freshly baked dough and cheese wafted through the air, mingling with the distant sound of traffic. Confident that he wasn't mistaken, as he was still wearing the suit, he decided to enter the pizza parlour and inquire about how long the shop next door had been empty.

A young man behind the counter was looking at his mobile. Upon noticing Lenny's entrance, he put the phone down and smiled. The scent of garlic and oregano surrounded him, and the hum of a nearby oven could be heard.

"How can I help you today?" the man asked, standing by the till, ready to take his order. His apron was splattered with tomato sauce and flour.

"Apologies, I don't require any food, just some information about how long the shop next door has been vacant," Lenny inquired, hoping the man could provide some clarity on the situation. He felt a slight chill as the door closed softly behind him, sealing off the outside noise.

The man looked at Lenny with a confused expression, as if Lenny had just made an unusual request.

"The shop has been closed for about six or seven years now," the man replied, resuming his focus on his mobile while leaning back against the counter, the screen illuminating his face.

Lenny thanked the man and walked back into the street, still confused about the charity shop's sudden disappearance. He was sure that the shop had always been there, with its bright blue sign and faces of happy children on its windows. Its sudden absence felt like a gap in his memory, as if a piece of the puzzle was missing.

On his way home, he decided to call Fran to thank him for his advice and see if he was free to catch up over a pint or two. He found Fran's number and pressed call. A woman answered.

"Hello?" she said, her voice tinged with suspicion.

"Hi," Lenny replied, "Sorry to bother you, could I speak to Fran please?"

"Who is this?" the woman asked, her tone hardening.

"My name is Lenny. We've been friends with Fran for a long time. I wanted to thank him for the advice he gave me on Friday," Lenny explained.

"You couldn't have spoken to Fran on Friday. He died two years ago in Malta. Can you please get your facts right before trying to scam me?" she snapped, and then hung up.

Lenny stood there, stunned and feeling sick. First, the charity shop vanished, and now he learned Fran had died. He felt like he was losing his mind. As he wandered home, trying to piece everything together, his thoughts raced. How could Fran have given him advice? Did he imagine the conversation? As he reached his house, the familiar sights of his neighbourhood seemed alien, distorted by his confusion. He sank down onto his sofa, head in hands, desperately searching for any logical explanation that could make sense of these bizarre events.

There are times in life when assistance from those who are no longer with us might be considered. If you find yourself without support and have dedicated your life to helping someone you care about, seeking help from past experiences or memories may be an option if no one else is there for you to turn to.

In such moments, reflecting on the advice, wisdom, and lessons imparted by those who have passed can offer valuable insights. Their words and actions might provide guidance during difficult decisions or challenging situations. Additionally, recalling shared stories or experiences can offer solace and encouragement, reminding you of the strength and resilience you possess. While their physical presence is absent, their influence and impact on your life continue to shape your journey, offering a unique form of support that transcends time.

Chapter 10
Bitter Chocolate

Crumpling's Newsagents is a small convenience store situated in Court Thorpe, a busy little town in the Midlands. The shop has been under the ownership of the Crumplings for many years, with husband and wife, Billy and Iris, managing it jointly. Although they did not have children of their own, they treated the local youngsters who frequented the shop as if they were family. The shop offered a wide range of essentials, from newspapers and magazines to household items and confectionery, making it a beloved spot for the community.

Despite the demands of early openings and late-night closing, they found joy in running the shop. Billy was known for his jovial nature and enjoyed chatting with the customers. Sometimes, he would crack a joke or two or play tricks on the younger customers, while Iris was meticulous in keeping the shelves well-stocked and tidy. Unfortunately, four years ago, Billy passed away, leaving Iris to manage the shop independently. Initially, she encountered difficulties, particularly due to her age of sixty-five, which made it a challenge to keep up with the physical demands of the job. Nevertheless, Iris's dedication to the shop and the community kept her going.

Everything appeared to be going smoothly, and she seemed to be managing well, especially with the help of Mr. Ghiram Sharma, who owned the shop three doors down. Mr. Sharma would go to the cash and carry for her and even helped with the banking. However, recently a new issue emerged: shoplifting, which became persistent and troublesome. Iris and Billy had dealt with shoplifting in the past, but not to the extent that Iris was suffering now. Despite her experience, Iris was struggling to find solutions to combat this issue. One night, Iris had trouble sleeping as she was aware that some customers were stealing from her. She realised that she could not afford security cameras and that putting up notices would not be effective. The shoplifting incidents were creating a financial strain on the shop, threatening its survival.

Determined to protect her shop, Iris began to implement measures. She rearranged the layout to ensure better visibility of certain items and to monitor them closely. Despite her efforts, she encountered resistance. She confronted a few shoplifters but was met with physical aggression and verbal abuse. The incidence of theft was increasing daily. Consequently, she ceased selling wine and beer, as those items were frequently stolen.

One afternoon, a smartly dressed man entered the shop. The shop was warm and welcoming, with a few customers waiting to be served. Initially, he browsed through the neatly arranged shelves that held an array of tinned foods, while Iris attended to other customers. The soft murmur of conversation and footsteps added to the lively atmosphere. When Iris had served all the customers, she turned her attention to the man. He looked about thirty and was wearing an expensive grey suit, white shirt, and a dark-coloured tie. Iris noticed the curiosity in his eyes.

"Good afternoon, sir. Is there anything I can assist you with?" Iris asked, maintaining a professional demeanour, her friendly smile inviting him to engage.

"Good afternoon to you, Mrs. Crumpling. You may not be able to assist me, but I might be able to assist you," said the man as he returned a bottle of milk to the refrigerator, took a handkerchief from his pocket and wiped his hands, then walked over to the counter where Iris was waiting with a puzzled look on her face. The shop was quiet; only the hum of the refrigerator and the rumble of traffic outside broke the silence.

"I understand you may have a significant issue with shoplifting, and I hope I can offer some assistance. My name is Jason Dresswick, and I believe I have the perfect solution to your problem," continued Jason, leaning on the counter and smiling warmly at Iris. His confident demeanour contrasted with the worry lines on Iris's forehead as she listened intently, hoping for a breakthrough in her ongoing struggle with theft in the shop.

"Please note, I cannot afford security cameras, and I don't wish to place my stock behind glass cases," replied Iris, her demeanour turning defensive. She felt she was already losing money due to the shoplifting, and now a man had entered her shop with the intent to sell her something.

"May I stop you there, Mrs. Crumpling? Be assured that I am not here to sell you anything. I am genuinely here to address your problem, and my solution requires no financial investment from you. I have something that will put an end to your shoplifting issues, and I believe you will find my proposal interesting," Jason said with a smile. He walked over to the greeting cards display, picking up some cards as he continued speaking to Iris. "When you close tonight, I will return for a meeting in the shop. How does that sound?" Jason asked as he moved around the shop, examining various items.

"Now, what exactly do I need to do? I'm not interested in selling my shop, and you mentioned that you do not seek payment of any kind. What is it that you want?" inquired Iris, looking more confused than ever as she approached where Jason was standing.

"All I require is a promise, a golden promise and a handshake, Mrs. Crumpling," said Jason, looking at Iris, waiting for her next question.

"A golden promise and a handshake? Your request is confusing to me, and I have a busy day ahead. Therefore, if you don't mind, please either buy something or leave," responded Iris firmly as she turned away from Jason and headed back to the counter.

"What I can offer you will help stop most of your shoplifting. There is no money involved and no need to sell your shop. You can remain here as long as you wish, but I must have a golden promise from you. Please consider it, and I will return tonight at eight," said Jason as he picked up a packet of mints and placed a five-pound note on the counter. "Please keep the change," Jason added as he left the shop.

Iris picked up the money and watched Jason leave the shop. She contemplated the nature of Jason's request for a significant commitment. Would he want to take over the shop, or perhaps require Iris to handle financial transactions covertly? Whatever his intentions, the prospect of experiencing fewer instances of shoplifting was appealing. Iris recorded the sale in the till and proceeded to the storeroom to retrieve tins of beans and boxes of crisps to replenish the shelves. While she was in the storeroom, she heard the bell above the shop door jingle.

"I'll be right with you," Iris called out as she returned to the shop, carrying a box of crisps with six tins of beans balanced on top.

"It's only me," said Mr Sharma, waiting by the counter.

"Good afternoon, Mr Sharma. How are you today?" inquired Iris as she placed the box down.

"I am very well, thank you, Mrs Crumpling. I'm heading to the bank; is there anything I can assist you with?" asked Mr Sharma, approaching Iris to offer his help if required.

"I'm fine today, Mr Sharma, but may I ask you something, please?" Iris responded, straightening herself and rubbing her back with her right hand.

"You are welcome to ask me anything you wish. Whether I know the answer, well, that's another matter," Mr Sharma replied with a touch of humour.

"Have you ever heard of Jason Dresswick?" Iris inquired, hoping Mr Sharma could provide information about him.

"Jason Dresswick? I'm afraid I've never heard of him. May I know the reason for your inquiry?" Mr Sharma responded, appearing puzzled.

Iris then proceeded to explain to Mr Sharma the details of her earlier meeting with Jason Dresswick and what he had suggested. Over the next twenty minutes, Iris explained everything to Mr. Sharma.

"Would you like me to be present tonight?" inquired Mr. Sharma, expressing concern regarding Iris's meeting with Jason Dresswick.

"No, I'll be fine. If anything were to happen to me, you will have the name of the man to provide to the police," responded Iris, still feeling uncertainty about her meeting with Jason.

"Please do not hesitate to call me if you require any assistance," Mr. Sharma advised before bidding farewell and departing.

Throughout the remainder of the day, Iris dealt with a steady stream of customers and attempted to apprehend several shoplifters. She took a break by closing the shop for about twenty minutes to eat and rest. Her thoughts were preoccupied with Jason and the nature of this so-called 'Golden Promise' he sought from her. As the time approached half past seven, Iris eagerly anticipated closing the shop. Back when Billy was alive, the shop would remain open until ten-thirty. However, Iris now closed at eight, and she felt a lot safer with this arrangement. While sweeping the floor, she was interrupted by the bell above the shop door jingling. She turned to see who it was and saw Jason walking in, carrying a large dark green bag in one hand.

"You're early, Mr Dresswick," said Iris as she leaned the broom against the counter.

"I'm only fifteen minutes early, that way I can show you how to stop shoplifters and explain a few things, and then the rest of the evening is yours. And please, call me Jason," he responded, making his way into the shop and placing his bag on the counter.

"I will be with you shortly; I need to clean the shop and ensure everything is prepared for tomorrow," replied Iris, bending down to pick up a pile of dirt with a dustpan and brush.

"No worries, I'm in no rush. Is there anything I can assist you with?" Jason asked, removing his jacket and placing it on the counter.

"No, I'm fine. I have a routine that I prefer to stick to. If anyone helps me, it disrupts my process. Please wait there, and I'll be free in a moment," Iris said, putting the dirt in the bin and then stowing away the cleaning equipment.

By about five to eight, everything was neat, ready for the next day. Iris walked over to the shop door, turned the sign to "closed," and locked and bolted the door.

"Would you like a cup of tea or a coffee, Jason? While we talk," Iris asked, walking towards the back of the shop.

"I'm not planning to stay for long. I want to explain something, and then I'll show you the product that will help you with your problem," Jason replied, loosening his tie.

"Alright, let's talk. I recall you mentioning that no money is involved, correct?" Iris asked as she walked behind the counter and sat on a stool.

"That's correct, no money involved whatsoever. What I do want is that golden promise and a handshake. I'll explain everything to you, and then show you the product after I get both of what I've asked for. Is that clear, Mrs Crumpling?" Jason replied, grabbing his bag and then waiting for Iris's response.

"There's no paperwork to sign, just a golden promise and a handshake. May I ask who you work for?" Iris inquired, looking increasingly confused. She was considering the possibility that this might be some scam, although she wasn't sure of its nature.

"The company I represent is Apollyon Ltd, and we aim to assist people in difficult situations by making their lives easier. That's why I'm here. We've received reports that shoplifting has become problematic in several stores in this area. Our sole intention is to help you, Mrs Crumpling," Jason replied, attempting to gauge Iris's reaction.

He could see that she was contemplating his words, deep in thought.

"Shoplifting has increased, and I'm losing stock nearly every day.

I do wish Billy were here to help me understand this," Iris said as she stood and walked over to the window of the shop. She stood there, watching all the people passing by, each with their own issues. Some hurried home to their loved ones, while an elderly couple strolled with their dog, holding hands and laughing. The evening sun cast a golden glow on everything it touched, creating long shadows that danced on the pavement.

She then turned, looked around her shop, and then glanced over at Jason. "Alright, I've made my decision. What is this golden promise I must swear by, and what is the product you have to show me?" Iris asked as she returned to her stool. Her voice carried a mix of apprehension and determination, her eyes reflecting the weight of the choice she was about to make.

"You've made the right choice, Mrs Crumpling. The golden promise is straightforward: you must never give this product to the innocent or disclose its existence to anyone, not even Mr Sharma. If you do, I will return and explain the consequences," Jason explained, extending his hand for Iris to shake. His face was stern, almost emotionless, but there was a hint of something deeper in his gaze — perhaps a history he didn't want to reveal.

Iris hesitated for a moment before shaking his hand, feeling the coolness of his touch against her warm skin. The gravity of the situation weighed heavily on her shoulders, but she steeled herself, knowing that this decision could alter the course of her life and her business. As their hands parted, a silent agreement settled between them, binding them in an unspoken contract, fraught with risks and secrets yet to unfold.

"Very good. Now, this is the product," Jason retrieved four large slabs of chocolate from his bag and placed them on the counter.

"This particular chocolate is intended solely for the shoplifters. You must not distribute it to anyone else, including yourself. Once ingested, they will experience a brief convulsion, followed by shrinking down to five inches in height, transforming into chocolate figures within seconds. These chocolate people you can now sell for, let's say, twenty pence each. Maybe more. Do you understand, Mrs Crumpling?" he inquired, with a satisfied expression on his face, just like the cat that got the cream.

"What have I agreed to?" Iris appeared startled, then covered her mouth with her hand. "This is incorrect and highly inappropriate. It could result in legal consequences," Iris responded, looking down at the floor. The whole situation was making Iris feel sick, and her head began to spin.

"Now listen to me and listen very carefully. Starting tomorrow, break the chocolate slabs into small pieces and put them in a bowl. Do not leave it out. Keep the bowl behind the counter, only offering it to the shoplifters, no one else. Tell them, if they can guess the flavour and get it right, they can have something for free for the rest of the week." Jason explained, his voice smooth and calming, like silk.

"Yes, I comprehend the entirety of this arrangement and assure you that I will not disclose it to anyone. I understand the consequences if

I give it to someone other than a shoplifter," Iris responded, her voice slow and measured. She appeared to be in a trance, her eyes distant.

Jason concluded the meeting by stating that every nine weeks, someone would deliver more chocolate. He elaborated on how this new arrangement was expected to reduce the number of shoplifters. With a confident air, Jason then picked up his jacket and bag, looked at Iris, smiled, unbolted the door, and left, leaving behind an aura of satisfaction.

Iris remained seated for a few minutes, processing what had just happened. She replayed Jason's words in her mind, feeling a mix of relief and dread. Realising she had made an error in judgment during the meeting, she understood it was too late to change things now.

Her thoughts turned to her late husband, Billy, and she wondered what he would have said if he knew about her actions. She pictured Billy's disappointed face. The weight of her decisions bore down on her as she sat in the empty shop, the silence amplifying her anxiety.

The following day, Iris opened the shop, despite feeling fatigued from a restless night. She felt unsure about offering a bowl of chocolate pieces to shoplifters. With numerous thoughts occupying her mind, she prepared a strong mug of tea, located a bowl, and began breaking the chocolate into bite-sized pieces.

The first few hours proceeded smoothly, with a consistent stream of customers and a few individuals who were merely browsing. At about 2:40 PM, a young teenager entered the store. Iris recognised him as a known shoplifter due to their prior encounters.

"Excuse me, young man, may I have a word with you, please?" Iris asked, trying her hardest not to appear frightened.

"What do you want?" he snapped. "I haven't done anything wrong. You lot always seem to be targeting us teenagers. I just came in to get a drink," the teenager grumbled, muttering under his breath.

"I simply want to offer you the opportunity to receive something free for a week. If you're not interested, I'll provide it to someone else," Iris replied, smiling gently at the lad, trying to keep her voice calm.

"What do you mean by 'free'? Nothing comes without a cost, Grandma, and I mean nothing. I'm not going to tidy up the shop or wash your car, understand?" he snapped again, beginning to walk towards the counter, looking confused.

"No, that's not what I meant. There's no tidying up or washing anyone's car involved. All you need to do is try this new brand of chocolate and identify its flavour. If you guess it correctly, you can have anything in the shop for free for a week. It's that simple," Iris explained, offering the bowl of chocolate to the lad.

"So, if I taste a piece of chocolate and correctly identify the flavour, I can have anything for free for an entire week?" the lad asked, watching the bowl and then looking up at Iris.

Without hesitation, the young man grabbed a piece of chocolate and popped it into his mouth. In a matter of seconds, his eyes widened, and he jerked slightly before disappearing. Iris rushed around to the front of the counter, and upon inspecting the floor, she found a chocolate figure resembling the young lad. It was about five inches tall, with intricate details, such as his baseball cap and baggy jeans.

Iris promptly picked it up, brushed it off, and placed it under the counter. She smiled to herself and murmured, "This is just the beginning. Many more to come."

By the end of the day, Iris had successfully created four more chocolate figures. More could have been made, but a rush of customers had arrived, and she decided to let them go, confident they would return.

As time went on, Iris's collection of chocolate people grew. There was a chocolate figure of a woman caught trying to steal a magazine and some tins of food, and a chocolate figure of a man trying to steal a couple of bottles of apple juice. While some might have seen her actions as cruel, Iris saw it as justice, a way to protect her livelihood. She had told them time and time again not to steal from her shop, but they refused to listen.

Reports began circulating that people were going missing. They were seen on CCTV moving around the town, but never seen leaving. The police suspected the possibility of a serial killer, prompting plans for searches in the local park and woods. Some locals thought it could be an alien abduction. The disappearances caused considerable alarm, leading to increased vigilance and a surge in reports of suspicious activity. Some even claimed to have seen strange lights hovering over the park.

The police conducted extensive interviews with residents and reviewed hours of surveillance footage in an attempt to identify patterns or potential suspects. Authorities also set up a dedicated task force to focus on the case, coordinating efforts with neighbouring districts to widen the search area.

Local media outlets picked up the story, urging anyone with information to come forward while advising caution and encouraging people to travel in groups or stay indoors after dark.

Everything was going well until one day Iris dealt with a shoplifter and left the bowl on the counter. She forgot to put it away, and while she was restocking the shelves, a woman came into the shop to buy a newspaper. While waiting, the woman helped herself to what she perceived as a free sample of chocolate. By the time Iris returned, the woman had turned into a chocolate figure. Iris picked her up and immediately started to worry, recalling Jason's advice: "No innocent people."

Iris swiftly placed the chocolate figure among the others, then seated herself on the stool, contemplating her next steps and the potential repercussions if Jason discovered what she had done. Without a phone number to reach him, she had no way to contact him, and there were no witnesses in the shop at the time, making it unlikely that Jason would find out.

Iris continued her duties as usual, serving customers and exchanging stories with regulars. At about seven-thirty, she began cleaning the shop and preparing everything for the next morning. When the bell jingled above the door, Iris turned around, and her heart skipped a beat. Standing before her was Jason. He appeared pale, and his eyes had a faint red hue. He walked into the shop and approached Iris.

"What have you done? Can you not recall what I instructed you? Your actions must have consequences," Jason's voice was cold, his gaze cutting through Iris as though he could see into her very soul.

"But… but it was an accident. I completely forgot about the bowl. I meant to put it back, honest! You have to believe me, please!" Iris stammered, her voice breaking. She backed away from him, tears streaming down her cheeks. She stopped, collapsing to her knees, her body shaking as she begged for forgiveness.

"There is no forgiveness. You had your chance," Jason replied, his words final, chilling. He stepped forward, placing both hands on her head.

Then, everything went black. Silence. Stillness.

Iris awoke with a jolt, her body tense, the sterile smell of a hospital room assaulting her senses. The room was minimalistic, with white walls and a small barred window. As she looked down, she saw herself in a hospital gown. Confusion swirled inside her as she tried to process the sudden shift in reality. The door clicked open, and a nurse entered the room.

"Where am I?" Iris asked, her voice trembling, her eyes wide with confusion as she scanned the unfamiliar surroundings.

The nurse responded sharply, "Please, Iris, not today. We do this every day. You know where you are—the same place you've been for the last four years." The nurse placed a small silver tray on the bed, containing four tablets, a plastic cup of water, and a hypodermic needle.

"I need to know where I am and where Jason Presswick is. I was in my shop—where is my shop? I need to go home now. You can't keep me here!" Iris exclaimed, desperation lacing her voice. She tried to sit up, anxiety pooling in her chest as her eyes darted around, searching for any hint of familiarity.

The nurse, a woman with tired eyes and a gentle yet firm demeanour, placed a hand on Iris's arm. "Listen, I'll explain this to you one more time. Now, get back into bed," she said, guiding Iris back onto the mattress and pulling the sheets over her.

"Iris, you are in Apollyon Mental Hospital," the nurse continued, her voice steady but matter-of-fact. "You've been here for four years. You killed your husband by poisoning him with chocolate. You never had a shop. You have no one who visits you, no family, no friends. When Dr Jason Presswick or Dr Oirat Lharma have finished their rounds, one of them will see you later. Now, please stop all this nonsense."

Iris's world tilted. Her complexion turned pale, her body frozen in disbelief. Her eyes were unfocused, her thoughts spinning. Could it be true? She had always believed in the existence of her shop, her life with Billy, the small victories and struggles of running the store. But the nurse's words rang in her ears, a cold, undeniable truth that sent a shiver through her.

The questions surged through her mind: Was it possible that everything she remembered—the shop, the customers, her life with Billy—had been a delusion? Had she truly poisoned him, or was it all a creation of her fractured mind? Was her reality slipping through her fingers?

The human mind, Iris realised, is an unpredictable labyrinth. How could she discern what was real from what was imagined? Was her life, her memories, all a mirage? The line between illusion and reality seemed so thin, so fragile now.

As she lay in the sterile room, her heart heavy with confusion and dread, Iris understood that she needed answers. But more than that, she needed to understand herself, to piece together the truth from the fragments of her mind. What was real? What had she done? And what would happen if she finally accepted that her memories might not be hers at all?

For now, all she could do was wait. The nurses, the doctors—they were the ones who held the key to her future. Would they show her the truth? Or would she remain locked in this place, forever unsure of her own reality?

Chapter 11
What goes around

Craig Tatum began his career from humble beginnings and gradually advanced through dedication and perseverance. He started out living in a small bedsit, where he often struggled to make ends meet, sometimes skipping meals and working multiple jobs just to pay the rent. The cramped conditions, limited privacy, and constant noise made it difficult to focus on his ambitions. Yet Craig dedicated every spare moment to learning new skills, networking within his industry, and saving whatever money he could.

Through years of self-improvement and persistence, he eventually achieved success by securing a penthouse flat in a converted warehouse beside the River Thames. The shift from humble lodgings to a luxurious apartment overlooking the city was both literal and symbolic of Craig's journey. This progression took nearly seventeen years, reflecting Craig's commitment to his goals and his ability to set long-term plans in motion despite setbacks.

As is often the case, periods of prolonged stability can signal underlying issues. A few difficulties are necessary to remain grounded. However, Craig viewed his journey differently—he endured significant hardships early on, such as financial uncertainty and loneliness, and now was prepared to embrace his achievements. Instead of feeling uneasy with stability, Craig welcomed the peace and comfort that came with his success, believing he had earned the right to enjoy his accomplishments after years of adversity.

One afternoon, Craig finished work and burst out of his office, his footsteps echoing sharply against the pavement as he darted towards the Underground. Breathless and impatient, he fumbled in his pocket for his train ticket, his eyes fixed ahead but blind to the world around him. He never saw the frail elderly woman crossing his path until his shoulder struck her with brutal force.

The elderly woman crumpled to the ground, a sharp cry escaping her as she clutched her knees and her wrist in pain.

"Out of the way, you silly cow," Craig snapped, his voice cutting coldly through the air. He didn't slow, didn't even look back, and was gone into the crowd.

For a long, chilling moment, the woman lay on the pavement, her breath shallow, her eyes darkened and glistening with something more than pain. Then, almost to herself, she whispered, her voice like the rustle of dried leaves:

"Tonight, and every night, your rest is over. I will be there, waiting."

A man and a woman nearby hurried to her side, lifting her gently, but neither could shake the strange chill that seemed to linger in the air long after Craig had vanished into the Underground station.

Craig walked into his flat, feeling the cool air brush against his face after a long day. He headed straight for the bathroom, letting the hot water wash away the stress before selecting a crisp pale blue shirt and a pair of dark jeans from his wardrobe.

When he met his colleagues at the lively downtown restaurant, laughter and animated conversations filled the table as they shared pizza and toasted with ice-cold beers. As the night wore on, Craig felt mild buzz from all the beers, his eyelids growing heavy. Realising it was late, he excused himself and stepped outside, breathing in the fresh night air during his walk home.

At home, he tossed his keys onto the oak side table near the front door and staggered past the quiet lounge. In his bedroom, he neatly folded his jeans and shirt over a chair, drew back the duvet, and settled comfortably onto the soft mattress, sighing with relief as fatigue overcame him.

Craig's breathing rasped softly in the darkness, his snores barely masking the hum of traffic beyond the window. On the bedside cabinet, the clock glowed with merciless clarity—2:45 a.m. The duvet twisted around his legs as the window blind rattled faintly in the warm night breeze.

The corner of the room swelled with movement. Shadows bled across the floor, thick and slow, until they gathered into a shape.

She drifted closer to the bed.

Moonlight kissed her features. Strands of grey hair hung like clotted string, slick with filth. Her skin sagged from her skull in folds, stretched thin and translucent in places, so that veins pulsed faintly beneath. Her nostrils flared wide, inhaling greedily, and a string of saliva trembled at her lip before breaking and falling wetly onto the quilt with a soft pat.

Then she smiled. Her mouth gaped broadly, blackened teeth jutted like broken shards of iron, sharp edges splitting her gums, dark blood oozing as if the act of grinning itself wounded her.

Her eyes wept a slow, thick fluid that streaked down her cheeks. Yet Craig could feel her gaze pressing into him, clawing at his dreams.

She leaned closer, her breath a stench of rot and earth, dripping onto his skin as her head tilted unnaturally to one side, vertebrae cracking like dry sticks. No sound followed—just the wet, bubbling, eager sensation—as though something inside her throat was struggling to crawl free. She climbed slowly onto his chest.

Craig stirred, his eyelids fluttering like moth wings. Panic surged through him, sharp and immediate. He tried to scream, to thrash, but his throat was locked, his limbs were dead weights. He was pinned inside his own body.

Her hands came down on his shoulders. Not soft, not warm— knobs of bone wrapped in papery skin. Each finger pressed deep, grinding into muscle, as though her skeleton itself was clawing its way into him. She lowered her head. The stink of rotten breath and decaying gums spilled over him. Her lips, cracked and dry, brushed the edge of his ear.

"Wqhhhhhhh," she croaked. Her voice sounded like a broken reed pipe.

Then it came—the slick, obscene drag of her tongue across his cheek. It was swollen, rubbery, grey, as if it had been soaking too long in stagnant water. The taste of decay clung to his skin.

"If you could scream now, I'd rip your skin off, but you can't," she laughed.

Her words vibrated with splatters of spit and blood against his jaw. Then her hand slid to his chest, cold, flat on his sternum. He felt the brittle bones beneath her skin shift and grind as she pressed down. The pressure grew, sharp and insistent, as though she meant to push straight through his flesh and snap his bones.

Her nails pressed into him, cold and deliberate, sliding between his ribs as if his body offered no resistance at all. He could feel them probing deeper, brushing the frantic beat of his heart. His pulse faltered, staggered, each beat weaker than the last. His vision dimmed—and then nothing.

The alarm screamed at 7:15 a.m. Craig lurched upright, heart hammering, lungs gulping air as though he had just surfaced from drowning. His hands clawed at his chest. No blood. No wounds. Just smooth, unbroken skin slick with sweat.

But the memory clung like smoke. The sensation of her weight on his chest, the press of nails, the dying flutter of his heart—it all felt too vivid, too solid to be a nightmare.

He sat trembling on the edge of the bed, staring at the pale lines of morning light creeping through the blinds. The thought whispered, unshakable: if it was only a nightmare, why does my chest still ache as if something is inside me, waiting?

Craig stood under the shower far longer than usual, letting the hot water scald his skin as if it might wash away the nightmare clinging to him. But when he pressed his hand to his chest, a dull ache pulsed beneath his ribs. It reminded him of his rugby days—of being slammed into the ground, air driven out of his lungs. Only this pain felt deeper, as though something had reached inside.

He forced himself through his morning routine—coffee, a rushed bowl of cereal, clothes pulled on without thought. But at work, concentration slipped through his fingers. The memory kept circling back—her rasping breath, the fetid stench that had crawled into his nose and stayed there. Every so often, he caught himself inhaling sharply, half-expecting to feel that decay against his skin again.

He laughed it off to colleagues at lunchtime when asked why he looked so tired. He explained his nightmare to them, muttering something about too much cheese on the pizza the night before, but the excuse rang hollow even in his own head.

When the day was done, Craig ducked into the pub for a couple of pints before heading home. A small ritual to take the edge off. If he could drink enough to soften the edges of memory, maybe he could convince himself it was just a stupid nightmare, nothing else.

Upon entering his home, Craig placed his keys on the oak side table before heading to the kitchen. The familiar scent of polished wood mingled with a faint trace of alpine air freshener, which sprayed every thirty minutes. He selected a few eggs, mushrooms, and tomatoes to prepare an omelette, methodically slicing the mushrooms and tomatoes and whisking the eggs, butter, and black pepper together as the pan heated up with a gentle hiss.

As the omelette sizzled, Craig retrieved a beer from the refrigerator—the cold condensation beading on his palm—and sat at the kitchen table, listening to the steady hum of traffic outside, blending with the occasional siren of an emergency vehicle going by. He savoured each mouthful, relishing the warm, hearty meal after his long day.

He spent the remainder of the evening flicking through sports channels. Craig skimmed through matches, occasionally cheering softly or shaking his head and swearing at a missed shot, the bright glow of the television reflecting across the room.

Afterward, he took a quick shower, letting the hot water ease the tension in his shoulders, before retiring to bed. The events of the day faded as he drifted off to sleep.

From the shadows in the far corner of the room, she drifted slowly forward, silent, deliberate. The air seemed to sink with her presence.

Her hands slammed against his shoulders, forcing Craig flat against the bed. She leaned over him, her face slowly moving toward his, her lips brushing his ear.

"Are you ready, my sweet child?"

She swung herself onto his chest, pinning him under her weight. Craig's eyes snapped open. He was awake—wide awake—but his body betrayed him. His arms refused to move, his voice locked inside his throat.

A cold sweat burst across his skin. He stared up as her face hovered closer, closer, her smile widening with every inch.

"I promised you'd never rest," she hissed. "And now I'll take your life apart—slowly, painfully."

Her hands crept over his ribs, skeletal fingers cold and rough, dragging like sharpened sandpaper. The nails—long, needle-thin—pierced through his skin, scraping along his ribs, sending bolts of white-hot pain tearing through his chest. Locked in silence, every nerve screamed as his blood welled beneath her touch. She lowered her head, creaking lips splitting as they pressed to his, dry and brittle, shaking against his mouth. The stench of rot filled him, choking, gagging, as if he were being forced to swallow decay itself.

Then came the tearing—her fingers sinking past flesh, prying through muscle, ribs creaking as if about to snap. His chest burned—not with fire, but with the sickening heat of something inside being pulled apart, stretched beyond breaking. Pain roared, drowning out thought, and as the wet sound of his own body giving way filled his ears, his mind surrendered to blackness.

He jolted upright, drenched in sweat, heart pounding so violently it hurt. For a frantic moment, he clawed at his chest, certain her fingers had been there, digging into him. He ripped the quilt aside and stared down at his body. No scratches. No bruises. Just skin slick with sweat.

But it didn't feel like his own.

The clock glowed: 5:15 a.m. The thought of closing his eyes again filled him with dread. Sleep was no longer safe. He showered, scrubbing his skin raw, but the water couldn't wash her away. Before leaving, he scribbled a shaky note to Jenny, his housekeeper, asking her to wash the bedding.

On the train, he sat rigid, eyes locked on the black void of tunnels.

But the glass betrayed him—her face stared back from the darkness, pale and unblinking. He whispered to himself that it was only a nightmare, only his mind playing tricks. Yet she slithered into every thought—the way she hunched over him, the rasp of her breath grazing his skin, the stench of rotting flesh clinging to her like a shroud. The smell clung to him still—sharp, rancid, undeniable. He pressed his sleeve to his nose, but it only made it worse, as if the stench had seeped into the fibres of his clothes, into his skin, into him.

He closed his eyes for a moment—only a moment—but he could sense that she was near, maybe standing in front of him, waiting for him to notice.

At work, Craig begged silently for the hours to drag, for the day to be longer and never end. The buzzing lights, the shuffling papers, even the endless drone of voices—these were shields against the silence of his apartment. He had loved his apartment once, but now the thought of going home and crossing its threshold made his stomach churn. He knew someone was waiting for him, and it was not a loving wife.

He clung to his friends over lunch, forcing laughter through a tight throat, pretending their company anchored him to the normal world.

But time was merciless. By 5:18 p.m., exhaustion pressed on his body, and he knew he could delay no longer.

He told himself that a few beers and a hot meal at his local restaurant might dull the edge, might drown the creeping terror long enough to let him collapse into a dreamless sleep.

But deep down, he knew better. Sleep was not rest—it was a hunting ground. And she would be waiting in the dark.

Craig managed to stumble through the front door just after eleven. As the lock clicked behind him, the apartment seemed to breathe—its shadows stretching long and heavy, swallowing him in silence. The air was thick, stagnant, and he could almost feel her waiting for him, somewhere in the dark, waiting for him to sleep.

He threw his keys onto the side table, the sound unnaturally loud in the silence of the apartment. Without wanting to linger in the hallway too long, he moved into the lounge and collapsed onto the settee. The television burst into life, a commercial about a man wanting his wife to spend more holiday time with him. It was the background noise Craig wanted, a fragile distraction from the oppressive silence pressing in from every corner of the room.

Eventually, he managed to drag himself into the bedroom. He stood at the door, swaying gently, his eyes sweeping the room again and again, looking for any movement or a silhouette in any of the dark corners. He pulled the window blinds tightly, shutting out the world, then sat on the edge of the bed and muttered hoarsely into the darkness, "Just leave me alone, bitch. Go and find someone else to play with and haunt their dreams."

Exhaustion pulled at him, but the fear he felt inside clung tighter. He pulled the duvet back and looked around the room one last time. His hand rested on the bedside lamp, then he decided to leave it on—a small guardian against the dark. In some way, he convinced himself that leaving the light on might just keep her away, or even stop his nightmares.

He adjusted the pillows, listened for a moment, and then fell asleep quickly. Within moments, his breathing softened, and then the snoring began. The lamp flickered a couple of times, dimming nearly into darkness. In its weak glow, she appeared.

She stood at the side of the bed, dressed in a filthy, tattered white dress stained with streaks of yellow and dark blotches. The material hung down like rotting flesh. The bedside lamp flickered once more, then stayed bright. The light revealed her face in merciless detail—her eyes sunken deep into her skull, her skin like leather, stretched tight and mottled in sickly shades of grey and green, as though embalmed.

She licked her dried, cracked lips and smiled as she leaned closer to Craig.

"Tonight, will be different, my sweet one," she whispered, then gave a little giggle.

"Tonight, I will let you talk," she said in a calm whisper that curled the air.

She placed her hands on the duvet and pulled it away with deliberate slowness, exposing Craig in his helplessness, as naked as the day he was born. Before Craig could react, she was straddling his chest, her weight pushing his body into the mattress. Craig's eyes opened wide, frozen with fear, feeling her cold, bony legs digging into his sides.

"You are mine," she laughed, licking her lips.

"You'll be my plaything, and I will show you how to respect others." Her jaw cracked as she smiled, and then she leaned close. Her lips started to split, weeping with a greenish pus, which trickled down to her chin. Then she leaned forward further and kissed him. The flesh of her tongue was soft and pulpy, like when you leave meat in direct sunlight to rot.

He gagged as she forced her tongue into his mouth, then he felt something hit the back of his throat, something wriggled, something thick. It was her tongue forcing its way down his throat. Her breath was like a corrosive vapour that burnt his tongue and ripped away the lining of his throat. Every swallow carried the taste of rotten flesh, iron, and rust. He could feel his own stomach twisting and burning.

She lifted her head and stared at Craig. Her lips started to quiver, and then her mouth began to froth violently, her lips peeling back as streams of blood and green pus frothed out, trickling down her chin.

The foul-smelling mixture sprayed across Craig's face. The stench of death filled his nostrils. He gagged and turned his head away.

"I haven't done anything to you! Stop this! Please, please!" he cried out in panic.

"You say you've done nothing, but you're wrong—very wrong," she hissed, grabbing him by his throat, digging her long, bony fingers further into his neck, tearing at his skin with such hatred. "I will make you regret the day you took your first breath. You, mister high and mighty, you think you're better than everyone else. You are nothing. Nothing but the scum under my fingernails."

"But... but I have never seen you before. Why do this to me?" He gasped, fear clawing at him. "You have this all wrong. I am not the man you want."

Blood and saliva washed over Craig as she laughed at him. "Oh, wrong. Wrong man. I have never been wrong, and you are the right man. You and no one else," she whispered, her voice dripping with malice as she drew her face closer to his. Then she laughed again, grabbing his head with both hands. The veins in the side of her neck, thick and black, bulged with effort, pulsing like a heartbeat beneath her leathery skin. Her foul-smelling breath poured over him, sour with rot and old secrets.

"Your mind remembers nothing, but your soul reeks of pomposity," she hissed. She flicked out her tongue, black and swollen, and licked his lips. "In your soul, there is a memory. A cursed memory. Of how you wronged me. And because of this, you now belong to me."

Craig's mind reeled as the air filled with her stench. He tried to wrench himself off the bed, but his limbs refused to obey.

The silence in the room deepened, her head tilting to one side, ears straining as though listening to something far beyond him. The shadows seemed to grow darker, twisting like smoke.

"Why have you been lying to me, Craig?" she said, not in his ear, but inside his head.

A cold shiver ran through his body. "What do you mean?" he thought, though no sound left his throat.

"All this was never earned by you. Your success was never hard-won. And those seventeen years of struggle... that was my struggle."

Craig's mind struggled to process her words, trying to grasp at their meaning. Then the room seemed to shatter. Memories, vivid and unwelcome, flooded his consciousness—the elderly woman he had knocked over, the chattering crowd, the glancing blow of his shoulder—flashes of other people, other accidents he had caused and just ignored in his haste for personal gain. Small things he'd done, collisions, cuts and bruises, a child left crying in the street. All of them, every single one, were his doing. His self-interest and carelessness had left pain and despair behind.

Her nails pressed deeper, but not into his body—into his mind. His body convulsed, writhing, twisting, until his body no longer felt like his own. His world blurred.

"I am your pain, the sum of all those you wronged and ignored," she laughed. "All those wrongs are now your pain. I am patient. I am eternal. And now, after many years, you belong to me."

Craig tried to resist, but the weight pressing down on him wasn't physical. It was guilt—years-old and merciless—sinking into him like acid. And as he finally screamed—a sound muffled by layers of his own conscience—the room fell silent, and then it descended into darkness.

When he finally opened his eyes, he was no longer in his penthouse flat. The air around him was colder, damp, and foul-smelling.

He was lying on the pavement, seventeen years younger, his shoulder aching, his eyes wide with panic. All around him, crowds of people passed by, not even noticing him.

On the other side of the road, standing still, was a frail elderly woman. She looked familiar to him. She raised her hand—not in greeting, but as a warning.

Craig realised with sickening clarity: he had never escaped. The life he thought he had earned, the success he had built with sweat and ambition, had been nothing but a hallucination—a dream conjured by the woman he had knocked over in the street. His real life had been left behind, the consequences of his arrogance piling up like corpses, each one feeding her power. He was now forced to walk in shadows forever, reliving every cruelty, every careless act, while she waited. Always waiting, to remind him: rest is not right. Rest is the punishment of the undeserving.

The final, crushing revelation hit him like a brick. The elderly lady fed his mind with one last thought. Craig saw himself sprawled and broken, every sin mirrored back in the rot of her smile. He screamed, but it was too late. The nightmare had claimed him, and he would never wake again.

Chapter 12
The Lost Tomb

Dr. Helena Amir stood at the edge of the western desert, shielding her eyes from the intense Egyptian sun. The sky overhead shimmered with heat, and mirages danced faintly along the horizon. Dust clung to her boots and canvas trousers, testimony to the hours spent trekking through the arid expanse.

The wind moved across the dunes, carrying subtle traces of the region's extensive history—whispers of ancient caravans and silent memories buried beneath shifting sands. Every distant call of a desert hawk or echoing footfall seemed woven into the very fabric of the landscape.

Dr. Amir relied not solely on observation but also on instincts developed over many years of archaeological work. Her expertise was born from decades of painstaking excavation in harsh conditions, field journaling under starlit skies, and decoding inscriptions in dimly lit tented camps. Each artifact unearthed was a testament to her patience and determination.

Throughout her career, she had discovered ancient tablets, pharaohs' tombs, and remnants of lost cities. Her name was well known among Egyptologists, her discoveries frequently featured in academic journals and museum wings.

However, the prospect of uncovering the so-called *Cost Chamber of Thutmose*—a site often regarded as purely mythical—presented a unique challenge. Legends described it as the resting place of a forgotten dynasty's secrets, its treasures and knowledge hidden from both tomb robbers and historians for millennia.

Dr. Amir possessed a critical piece of evidence: an untranslatable glyph discovered beneath the deteriorating stones of Karnak Temple, which corresponded to a line found in a restricted scroll housed in the Cairo Museum archives.

The glyph was etched deeply, as if intended to outlast centuries of erosion. Its mysterious symbols hinted at directions—or perhaps a warning. She spent countless nights poring over high-resolution photographs, cross-referencing every mark against obscure dialects and long-lost scripts, determined to unlock the secrets that had eluded generations before her.

She had deciphered the initial part of the riddle. Next, she would venture further into the desert.

The sun shone intensely on the Oasisara plateau as Dr. Amir examined the entrance of a newly discovered shaft. She inspected the worn hieroglyphs carved into the stone lintel, her hands marked by years of archaeological work.

Beads of sweat collected on her brow beneath the cloudless sky, the heat radiating off the yellow limestone and shimmering across the sand. Helena knelt down, brushing away fine dust from the ancient symbols with delicate precision, her fingertips tingling at the possibility of what lay beneath.

The air was thick with anticipation and the faint scent of stone warmed by centuries of sunlight. As she compared the markings with sketches from her notebook, she considered how these inscriptions might relate to the riddle's clues—each line could unlock another layer of Egypt's buried history.

On the plateau, with only a falcon's call breaking the silence, Helena prepared to descend. The wind tugged gently at her jacket, and a faint scent of stale air drifted from the passage. They moved slowly through a cobweb-filled corridor lit by their torches. A gentle breeze blew between them and the damp, rough-hewn stone walls as dust motes floated in the air. They reached a small chamber with two entrances—one they had just come from, and one leading into darkness ahead.

Maintained echoes amplified every movement, making each footstep seem louder than it truly was. A stone inscribed with obscured symbols sat by the doorway, its surface worn smooth by centuries, suggesting secrets patiently waiting beneath layers of dust and cobwebs.

The symbols appeared to be ancient, likely predating the Old Kingdom tombs in the area, possibly originating from a predynastic period. The glyphs were carved deeply into the sandstone, their edges smoothed by millennia of drifting desert winds. Faint traces of ochre clung to their grooves, hinting at the colours they once bore.

Wusuf Gahri, Helena's assistant and translator, knelt beside the inscription, his torch trembling slightly in his grip as he traced the outline of the text. He read aloud, his voice echoing off the cool stone walls.

"It seems to say, *Beware the Breathless King. The seal must stay unbroken,* and below that it reads, *Doom unspoken.*" His brow furrowed, and he glanced nervously at Helena, uncertainty flickering in his dark eyes.

Helena, her eyes narrowed with determination, adjusted her battered hat and surveyed the passage ahead. She noted the subtle shift in the air, a dryness that prickled at her throat. Turning to the others, she instructed, "Gather the equipment. We will proceed." Her words rang with authority, but those closest to her could hear the undercurrent of anticipation and caution threading through her tone.

The passageway descended in a spiral with unusual geometry, reaching depths greater than any previous excavation. Its walls curved at odd angles, twisting the perspective in ways that unsettled the senses.

The air was stale and cold, tasting faintly of minerals and carrying a claustrophobic silence, broken only by the explorers' footsteps, which produced distinct, resonant echoes that seemed to linger longer than normal. At the base, there was a concealed chamber carved from black basalt, the stone surface glistening with metallic veins that pulsed dimly under their torchlight. The environment carried the scents of incense, ambergris, and myrrh, along with a sharp, electric odour reminiscent of ozone, which tingled in their nostrils with each breath.

In the centre stood a golden urn, its polished surface reflecting warped images. Taller than an average person, it was set with sapphires that caught and fractured the light into glimmering blue shards scattered across the floor.

Richalcum chains, thick and ancient, secured the vessel, their links etched with runes that shimmered subtly as if alive. The chains reflected every movement, casting erratic shadows along the chamber's perimeter.

Wusuf quietly spoke a prayer, his voice barely more than a whisper.

"This is wrong. Nothing beneficial is sealed like this." His hands shook slightly as he made a protective sign.

Helena, her brow furrowed in concentration, examined the urn, running her fingers just above the surface without touching it.

"Then why does it feel as if it's observing us?" Her gaze met Wusuf's, wide and uneasy, as a subtle pressure in the chamber intensified, pressing against them like a silent warning.

The lid of the urn was intentionally constructed to remain closed, secured by a strong seal. Engraved around its base were intricate runes, deeply inscribed into the gold—each serving as a warning, a prohibited invocation, or an urgent request. Nonetheless, apprehension alone proved insufficient to deter human curiosity.

Despite Wusuf's urgent objections, Helena disengaged the ancient locking mechanism with unsteady hands. A cold wind and a hissing sound resonated through the chamber, reminiscent of a serpent emerging from confinement, as an intensified darkness emanated from within the urn.

A thick column of black smoke erupted from the urn, twisting like a serpent toward the vaulted stone ceiling. It morphed into a towering humanoid form, constantly shifting between impenetrable darkness and swirling mist.

Its features blurred as if torn from nightmares, rimmed by flickers of unnatural fire. Its eyes glimmered with the dying light of distant stars, sending chills deep into their marrow. The chamber's temperature plunged, each breath tasting of dread as the dense air pressed in, suffused with the acrid stench of burnt flesh and ancient ash.

Though the figure uttered no words, a maelstrom of overlapping whispers—some pleading, others mocking—echoed relentlessly off the ancient stones, their dissonance gnawing at sanity. Helena staggered, her legs buckling as she dropped to the ice-cold flagstones, clutching her ears to fend off the cacophony. Her chest heaved with frantic, ragged breaths. Her vision swam with shadows and panic, every nerve screaming in response to the overwhelming, malignant presence that now filled the chamber.

The jinn, bound by the enchantments of the urn, could not leave the chamber unless its essence was carried by a mortal host. Its ethereal form hovered above the fractured stone floor, manifesting as subtle blue lights that flickered intermittently. Intricate patterns were inscribed on the walls, their surfaces shimmering in response to the jinn's presence, casting unusual reflections upon Helena and Wusuf.

Whispers of ancient magic seemed to echo through the cool air, carrying an undertone of longing and unrest. The jinn's blue lights pulsed, sometimes coalescing into ghostly shapes before dissolving again into misty trails. Dust hung suspended in the beams of light, sparkling as if charged with energy each time the jinn shifted.

The complex wall engravings glowed faintly, their lines threading across the stone in mesmerising, ever-shifting constellations. Helena's heartbeat quickened as shadows danced across her face, while Wusuf caught the faint scent of burnt incense and felt the hairs on his arms rise, sensing the weight of centuries-old secrets pressing in from all sides.

The jinn presented Helena with an offer: power, knowledge, and access to the secrets of the ancient world. Its ethereal form shimmered in the dim light, shifting between shapes both human and unrecognisable, and its voice echoed unnaturally through the domed chamber, causing dust to rise from the centuries-old carvings etched deep into the stone walls. Shadows wavered along the floor as the jinn spoke, the air thick with the scent of old incense and earth.

Though her heartbeat thundered in her chest and her hands shook at her sides, Helena declined the jinn's proposal. Her voice trembled but carried steady conviction as she met its intense, otherworldly gaze, refusing to be swayed despite the overwhelming pressure that seemed to press in from every direction.

Wusuf intervened.

"Your promises are deceitful, rooted in corruption. My study of ancient texts reveals you as the devourer of voices," he said, standing between Helena and the jinn, clutching a worn leather-bound tome close to his chest. Sweat beaded on his brow despite the chill that filled the air.

The jinn responded with a measured smile.

"If that is so, I shall simply take what I require." Its eyes glinted with cold amusement as it drifted closer, its form pulsing with dark energy.

The jinn moved forward, knocking the torches from their hands, landing on the other side of the chamber. The area became dark, and only a faint outline of the jinn could be seen as it proceeded. The air temperature dropped, and noticeable physical reactions occurred on Helena's skin. The jinn's whisper was audible from varying distances as it extended its hand toward them.

Helena found herself paralysed by the jinn's approach, the air vibrating with electricity and dread. Its presence pressed upon her mind, probing, sifting through memories and fears.

Wusuf stood his ground, voice trembling with a litany of prayers as he tried to shield them both with the ancient tome. The jinn's laughter— a soundless tremor—coiled around their thoughts, scattering Wusuf's words into fragments.

With a sudden, terrifying surge, the jinn extended a shadowed hand toward Wusuf. Wisps of blue light streamed from the tome, swirling around the jinn's outstretched fingers. Wusuf's voice faltered, his eyes wide with terror and resolve as he clutched Helena's arm.

"Run," he gasped, and everything fractured. The world erupted in cold, blinding light, a soundless explosion of agony and magic.

Helena's senses flickered. She glimpsed Wusuf, his silhouette wreathed in swirling shadows, the jinn's form enveloping them both. The chamber spun in a vortex of shrieking wind and burning sigils, the runes along the walls pulsing in desperate protest.

Something tore loose—an ancient seal, perhaps, or Wusuf's last desperate spell. Helena's body was flung backward, striking the cold flagstones. Pain blossomed up her spine as the world receded into darkness, the echo of Wusuf's name torn from her lips. For a heartbeat, everything was silent.

Helena drifted at the edge of consciousness, her senses battered, the oppressive weight in the room suddenly gone. She tasted ash, sand, and ozone in the dust and felt the faint pulse of magic settling like dust. She knew, in her bones, that the balance had shifted—the urn's occupant was no longer bound by ancient law.

Slowly, sound seeped back into the world: a low ringing in Helena's ears, the distant drip of water, the ragged heave of her own breath. Her vision swam, afterimages flickering—runes smouldering on the walls, the lingering shimmer of spectral blue, Wusuf's outline burned into her memory like a negative on film.

She pushed herself upright, pain lancing through her shoulders and ribs. The chamber was shrouded in a heavy, unnatural gloom. Where the jinn had once hovered, a swirl of luminous embers now hung suspended in the air, orbiting the battered urn.

The ancient tome lay open at Wusuf's feet, pages fluttering in an unseen wind. Helena's hands trembled as she reached for her friend, desperation clawing at her throat.

"Wusuf..." Her voice was barely more than a whisper, muffled by the oppressive hush. He knelt amid the dust and scattered fragments of runes, his face pale and streaked with tears. Around them, the sigils on the wall faded, their angry glow receding to a dull, exhausted glimmer.

For a moment, neither spoke. It was Wusuf who broke the silence at last, his voice hoarse and hollow.

"The seal has been broken," he said, and his eyes, rimmed red, flickered with something Helena could not name. "But it is not destroyed." His words faltered as the urn trembled, a faint new crack spiderwebbing across its surface.

Outside, a tremor shuddered through the sands. Dust rained down from the domed ceiling. Helena rose unsteadily, her heart pounding as she watched Wusuf gather the tome and clutch it to his chest, staggering upright. His hands moved over the runes in a frantic, searching pattern.

"We have only moments," he murmured. "It is not finished with us yet."

Beneath the surface, the jinn's laughter seemed to ripple through the stones, promising that the ancient struggle was far from over.

A chilling wind coiled through the chamber, carrying a hiss that was both voice and memory. Helena swallowed, steadying herself as she watched the swirling embers pulse and contract, as if breathing. The air vibrated with tension, thick with an energy that threatened to snap.

Wusuf's fingers halted on a single rune—cracked, faintly glowing. His breath hitched.

"This one," he whispered. "It's the binding sigil. If I speak it—"

A thunderous boom cracked overhead. Cracks webbed across the dome, letting in drifts of sand. Helena rushed to Wusuf's side, clutching his arm.

"What if you speak it wrong?"

The wind howled louder now, no longer just wind. It clawed at their clothes, tugged at the pages of the tome, and carried with it the scent of scorched wood and blood.

"I know," he said grimly, "but we're out of time."

Behind them, the stones began to shift. Not fall, but move—as if they were awakening.

Helena stepped back instinctively.

"Wusuf..."

But he was already chanting, his voice low and firm. The runes flared, and the jinn screamed—not in pain, but in delight. It was ready, and it remembered their names.

The scream twisted through Helena's ears like a blade of ice. She clapped her hands over her ears, but the scream wasn't just heard—it was also felt, vibrating in her bones, twisting through her spine.

Wusuf's voice wavered. The glow from the runes flared again, too bright now, casting monstrous shadows that danced across the walls. Embers spun faster in the air, forming shapes—half faces, clawed hands, screaming mouths—that vanished before they fully formed.

The stones behind them slid with a grinding moan. A shape, free from the wall, rose tall and sinuous, built of smoke, ash, and memories. Its face was a smooth mask of darkness, and beneath it, fire coiled like breath.

"Mortals, fools," it hissed, though its mouth did not move. "You disturbwhat cannot die."

Wusuf didn't stop. His chant rose in pitch, defiant and desperate. Sweat poured down his face, the sigil beneath his fingers now burning white-hot.

The jinn recoiled slightly, its form flickering.

"You cannot bind me again. The pact is broken. The gate is now wide open."

Helena stepped in front of Wusuf, hand outstretched—trembling but resolute.

"You may be ancient," she said, her voice slightly shaking, "but you still fear one thing."

The jinn drifted slightly forward, its head tilted, curious. "That one thing is being forgotten," continued Helena.

The chamber reacted instantly. The walls shivered, and a second wind surged in. The runes on the floor, untouched until now, lit up like a constellation.

Wusuf's eyes snapped open.

"She's right," he said hoarsely. "We don't need to bind it. We need to erase it."

The jinn screamed again, but this time there was an edge of panic. Helena lunged forward, her palm slamming onto the central sigil.

"Unname it, do it now!" Wusuf roared.

Together, they spoke the last word—a word no tongue had spoken in a thousand years. The chamber imploded with a flash of light, then silence. A stillness so absolute it rang in their ears.

Helena opened her eyes slowly, blinking against the afterimage burned into her vision. The chamber was… still. Dust hung in the air like mist. The swirling embers were gone. The runes were dark. Even the ever-present hum—the living tension beneath the stones—had vanished.

Wusuf was kneeling beside the tome, one hand splayed on its now-blank pages. Ash ringed the edges, as though the words themselves had been burned out of existence.

"Did we…?" Helena's voice broke. "Did we succeed?"

Wusuf didn't answer at first. He looked around slowly, as if seeing the chamber for the first time. There was no sign of the jinn. It had gone—no smoke, no shape, no heat. Only stone. Still cold.

"It's gone," he whispered. "I can't feel it anymore. No voice, nor breath." He placed his hand over his heart. "It's silent." He smiled.

Helena collapsed beside him, exhaustion crashing over her in a wave. Her hands were raw from where she had touched the sigil, faint burn marks tracing strange circular patterns into her skin.

"But where did it go?" she asked, though she almost didn't want the answer.

Wusuf shook his head.

"Not banished. Not bound. Unmade. We erased its name from the world. Without a name, it cannot be remembered. And without memory…"

"It ceases," Helena finished.

They sat in the silence, letting it hold them like a blanket. But even then, in the deepest quiet, there was a flicker of unease. Not fear, exactly—but awareness. They had performed something ancient, irreversible. Not a victory, a rewriting.

And somewhere far away, in a place without time or shape, a different name stirred.

Egypt had never seen so much rain. It had not stopped since Wusuf unmade the jinn.

Pillagers spoke in whispers, unwilling to say aloud, but Helena saw it in their eyes—the unease, the sense that something wasn't right. Crops yellowed in their soil. Birds flew in tight, frantic circles. At night, dogs howled and would not be comforted.

Wusuf had grown withdrawn, pouring over the now-blank tome, as if the missing words would reveal themselves in absence. His hands shook, and he hadn't slept.

"It wasn't supposed to have spread," he muttered one morning when Helena brought him food. "The spell should've been contained."

Helena leaned on the doorframe, watching him with growing concern.

"What do you mean by 'spread'?"

He looked up, his eyes red and puffy.

"We erased the jinn's name, yes. But in doing so, we may have torn something deeper. The threads of naming, Helena—they're not just words. They anchor things. And something's unravelling."

Outside, distant thunder rumbled. That night, the sky turned the colour of old bone, and a stranger arrived in the village. She wore a cloak darker than the night itself. It seemed to resist the lantern light. Her face was hidden beneath a veil, but her voice was clear.

"I seek the ones who undid the name," she said, standing in the village square. "Because you have now opened the gate beneath the gate."

Helena stepped forward, cold settling in her chest.

"Who are you?"

The stranger turned toward Helena.

"A witness. A keeper of the forgotten." She raised her hand. And the earth cried out—not with sound, but with a memory. A scream from below the roots of the world. Every stone and tree trembled.

Wusuf stumbled from his bed and stood behind Helena, gripping the doorframe. His mouth fell open.

"No... that's not possible. The name, we didn't erase one jinn. We erased an anchor."

The stranger nodded once.

"You've set something loose. And now... the forgotten will remember you." The world is changing. Not like the great flood or a great firestorm, but in absence."

Over the next few weeks, changes were happening across the world. Individuals lost the ability to articulate basic words—such as "stone," "sunlight," and "north." People would frequently hesitate during conversation, searching for terms that seemed to have vanished from memory.

Maps deteriorated as their ink seemed to evaporate from the page. Additionally, children were born without shadows and showed an inherent inability to acquire new knowledge.

Nations were undergoing significant transformations. The land was desiccating, and extensive fissures appeared, as though the territories themselves were separating. Beneath everything, a persistent vibration— a perceptible but inaudible tremor within the earth. Helena characterised it as a heartbeat devoid of a heart. The once-fertile ground now bore the appearance of parched parchment, curling at the edges as if recoiling from some unseen catastrophe. Air shimmered with heat and tension, while trees stood motionless, their leaves brittle and turning grey. People watched the changing world with fear and awe, whispering about omens and ancient prophecies.

Wusuf comprehended the true nature of the phenomenon upon discovering the glyph inscribed at the entrance of the passageway to the chamber. The stone itself was cool to the touch, marked by patterns that seemed to flicker at the edges. It was neither a rune nor a symbol, but rather a void rendered in form—a signifier defined by absence rather than presence. The shape drew the gaze into it, evoking a sense of loss impossible to name—a silent erasure where meaning should have been.

"It is not an organism," Wusuf explained to Helena that evening, his voice low just above a whisper as dusk settled around them. Shadows stretched along the cracked ground, echoing the unease within. "It is an act of forgetting, a force, utilising our cognition as its medium." His tone carried both dread and fascination, as if the knowledge itself threatened to vanish the instant it was spoken aloud, leaving only questions behind.

In the hills beyond the village, the trees had stopped growing. Instead, inversions appeared—places where tree-shaped holes pierced the sky, perfectly black, perfectly silent. Animals refused to go near them. The villagers began dreaming in a language no one could describe.

They woke with blank eyes and bleeding palms, clawing invisible symbols into walls and soil while they slept. Some tried to flee but only ended up back in the village.

And one morning, the stranger was waiting at Helena's door. She still wore the veil.

"You must come," she said. "It has breached its first threshold."

Helena didn't ask what it was. She already knew.

Helena and Wusuf accompanied the stranger beyond the village, passing through fields covered in white grass that did not move in the warm breeze. The grass glowed faintly in the dimming light, each blade seemingly frozen in time. The silence was heavy, amplifying the sound of their footsteps on the brittle ground.

They arrived at a round depression in the earth, resembling a hollow made with precision. The earth sloped gently downward, its edge marked by weathered stones streaked with dry moss. At the centre was a form—an indistinct void, encircled by stones from which water flowed in thin, silvery streams that seemed to vanish into nothingness.

The air above it felt icy cold, and a strange pressure built in Helena's chest as she drew closer.

From this area, voices could be heard. They were neither screams nor calls, but rather a continuous recitation of names—each one spoken, then fading immediately, disembodied and eerily rhythmic, like a litany carried on an invisible current. One name lingered on the edge of Helena's memory—unfamiliar yet somehow known to her, echoing with a haunting familiarity that unsettled her deeply.

She asked, her voice barely more than a whisper,

"What is that?"

The stranger looked at Helena, then at Wusuf, before

speaking, her tone solemn and distant.

"This is the first silence. The world will turn inward within a matter of hours. The unspoken god has awakened, and as a result, the world and everything upon it will cease to exist." Her words hung in the air, merging with the recited names, as if joining an ancient chorus bearing witness to the world's inevitable decline.

Helena felt a subtle unease creep through her. The atmosphere grew noticeably tense, as though anticipating an imminent development. In the dim light,

"What is the significance?" Helena inquired, her question fading into the prevailing silence.

The stranger's gaze flickered with something neither hope nor despair.

"It means that memory will become the last refuge. Every name you hear is both a reckoning and a farewell. In the end, only the names will remain. The world will start to pull itself in, and then just memories will remain."

A hush fell, deeper than before, as if the world itself were holding its breath. Helena strained to recall the name that hovered in her mind, desperate to tether herself to meaning, but it slipped away as the litany continued—relentless and serene. All around, the darkness listened, and the silence thickened with the weight of all that was about to be lost.

Certain items come with warnings advising that they should not be opened. However, human curiosity often compels us to explore the unknown, even when cautioned otherwise. Occasionally, this leads to the release of matters that, despite our best efforts, cannot easily be contained again. Sometimes, in seeking what is lost, we investigate further. The question remains: are we truly prepared for the consequences of our actions? I leave you to consider this thought.

Chapter 13
Room 247

Jenny Chalk had experience with ghost stories and every other paranormal tale you could think of. As a reporter for *The Night Walkers Sentinel*, she had examined cold cases, exorcisms, and even spent a week in a house in Derbyshire reported to have a poltergeist.

However, her assignment at the Fisherman's Inn was unlike anything she had experienced before.

Jenny prided herself on her methodical approach, often spending long nights combing through archives or interviewing witnesses who swore they'd seen something supernatural. She'd faced chilling drafts in derelict mills and mansions, deciphered cryptic diary entries, and even accompanied mediums during séances.

But the Fisherman's Inn posed new challenges: its haunting stories were entwined with local legends, whispered histories stretching back centuries. Tucked away on a fog-shrouded coast, the inn's creaking doors and salt-stained walls seemed to hold secrets no ordinary investigation could uncover. Jenny sensed that this assignment would test not just her journalistic instincts, but also her resolve—and perhaps her skepticism—in ways she hadn't yet imagined.

Situated upon the rugged Cornish coast, the inn seemed hewn from the very cliffs it perched upon. Its weathered stone walls blended seamlessly with the rocky outcrops, lending an air of permanence and resilience.

The study timbers, darkened by years of wind and salt, creaked and groaned whenever a strong wind swept in from the sea, as if voicing ancient secrets. The slate roof, mottled with patches of moss and lichen, bore scars from countless storms, its edges chipped and uneven.

Locals often recounted that the inn had endured over three centuries, surviving tempests and tales alike. Some would lower their voices, and, when pressed, mention Room 7UN—a room wrapped in whispers and wariness.

Jenny deliberately selected this room, relying on her extensive background in probing unsettling cases and unearthing cold, objective truths. Over the years, countless chilling reports had surfaced—echoes of screams piercing the dead of night, mysterious disappearances without a trace, all occurring in locked rooms where every door was bolted shut, and every window sealed tight. The only things left behind were wet puddles leading from the bathroom to the middle of the room.

Jenny methodically pinpointed this very room—the room that bred fear in anyone who entered, the room that had been the source of so many sinister accounts. She was determined to capture the evil darkness that lurked in the shadows.

Upon approaching the front desk, the smell of aged wood, old books, and a faint scent of salt filled the air. The mellow, golden glow from the wall lighting cast shadows along the oak countertop, where a register lay open with a pen resting beside it. An elderly man stood behind the counter, appearing to be around seventy years old, with a bald head framed by wisps of grey hair that curled slightly above his ears. His face was lined with deep-set wrinkles, and he wore a crisp white shirt beneath a buttoned black waistcoat, its fabric slightly worn but meticulously maintained. A gleaming brass watch chain peeked from his pocket.

When Jenny entered, he lifted his gaze with a reserved smile, his blue eyes attentive as he nodded politely in greeting.

"Good evening, miss. How may I help you?" he asked in a croaky voice.

"I have a booking for Room 7UN under the name Jenny Chalk," Jenny replied with a smile, placing her bags down.

He turned slightly pale, checked the guestbook, marked something next to her name, and handed her the book to sign.

"Are you quite sure about your choice of room, miss?" the concierge asked quietly, his voice edged with concern that seemed to echo the hush of the reception area.

As Jenny stepped forward to the counter, "Yes, Room 7UN, please," she caught the scent of his aftershave—it reminded her of camphor wood, with another smell lingering that she couldn't quite place. The elderly concierge's hands shook slightly as he slid the heavy guestbook towards her, his eyes darting nervously between the page and her face.

Behind him, an ornate clock ticked loudly, each second echoing against the wooden wall panelling. Jenny hesitated for a moment, noticing how his knuckles whitened as he gripped the pen before offering it to her. The shadows on the faded wallpaper added to the sense that something unspoken lingered just beyond the reach of the wall lights.

The elderly concierge paused briefly before handing her the brass key marked with the number 7UN on its wooden key ring. Their eyes met for a moment, during which Jenny noticed a subtle expression on his face, a mixture of caution and melancholy, perhaps tinged with something unspoken. She wondered if he, too, harboured memories or suspicions about what had transpired within these walls.

As Jenny tucked the key into her coat pocket, an uneasy hush seemed to settle over the reception, broken only by the distant creak of the floorboards, the worn carpet, and the ticking of the clock, along with the low murmur of the wind outside. With each step towards her room, she felt both anticipation and apprehension building, aware that tonight might reveal answers long buried in the shadows of time.

The further she walked along the hallway, the colder it seemed to get. The wallpaper was peeling at the edges, while small cobwebs glistened in the corners. The uneven floorboards creaked and groaned beneath her feet, and the smell of damp stone, mould, and a faintly sweet odour filled the air.

Her heartbeat quickened with each step she took. Pausing outside her room, she retrieved her key. She hesitated for a moment before sliding it into the lock, her fingers trembling slightly as they fumbled with the cold metal. For some strange reason, a wave of fear swept over her, accompanied by an overwhelming sense of sadness and apprehension. As the door opened with a creak, a gust of wind rushed past her, chilling her skin. From somewhere in the darkness of the room, the faint, haunting sound of a child crying drifted out, sending shivers down her spine and making her pause at the threshold.

She located the light switch and turned it on, filling the room with a dull yellowish light. She closed the door and placed the key in the lock. The room was furnished with an antique wooden dresser, its surface marred by shallow scratches, and there was a faint trace of furniture polish in the air. An iron bed with a thin, slightly sagging mattress stood against one wall, topped by a pink candlewick bedcover that showed gentle pilling from years of use.

The wallpaper featured faded floral patterns with curled edges, hinting at decades gone by, and in some places, the paste had loosened enough to create tiny gaps between paper and plaster. Pastel green curtains hung at the window, their fabric soft but holding a musty scent, barely diffusing the muted light from outside. A small wooden bedside cabinet stood next to the bed, supporting a lamp that leaned slightly, its shade crooked and dusty, casting an uneven shadow across the floor. There were no immediate signs of anything unusual, and the room was so silent that she could hear the faint sound of the floorboards creaking back into place. Even the air felt still, waiting for something to happen. ,

Jenny looked around the room. It was far from ideal, but it would do for one night. She set her bags on the squeaky bed, unpacked, and methodically placed her equipment: a voice recorder by the bed, cat balls at the door, and an infrared camera near the dresser.

After checking the batteries, she reviewed her setup, smiled, and called out,

"I'm ready for any spirits to come forward and let me know you're here with me."

Jenny's hands worked with practiced precision as she rearranged each device, careful not to disturb the dust-laden curtains. Satisfied with her careful preparations, she took a deep breath, feeling anticipation ripple through the stillness, and waited for a response in the charged air.

A creaking sound echoed in the hallway, followed by what resembled a whisper or a moan, and then another floorboard groaned amid faint murmurs. Jenny experienced a chill as goosebumps formed on her arms, the hairs standing upright as if sensing an unseen presence.

She paused, heart pounding, listening attentively for any further sounds or voices, her breath shallow and uneven. Cautiously, she proceeded toward the door, her footsteps tentative against the timeworn carpet. She carefully took hold of the cold, tarnished key and attempted to turn it. However, despite multiple efforts—jiggling, pulling, and twisting—the key remained stuck fast, heightening her sense of unease.

Each failed attempt seemed to amplify the oppressive silence around her, making the darkness feel heavier and the air colder than before.

Jenny paused by the door, her hand hovering uncertainly over the key as she glanced around the dimly lit room. Gathering her composure, she walked towards the infrared camera mounted on a tripod, its small red light blinking steadily.

"If that's your way of showing your presence, thank you," she said softly, her voice echoing slightly in the quiet room as she carefully adjusted the camera to face the door.

Jenny's brow furrowed in concentration as she ensured the lens was steady and in the right place.

"Can you tell me your name, please?" she asked, turning back and retreating towards the door, her steps slow and deliberate. The camera flickered, the feed briefly distorting as it refocused on her silhouette approaching the door, casting a long shadow across the floor.

She stood in absolute stillness for several minutes, though every second felt like an eternity. The air was thick with tension, and every faint tap and unexpected creak sounded unnaturally loud, as if the building itself was whispering secrets. With trembling hands, she pulled the voice recorder from her pocket and switched it on, her heart pounding in her chest.

Gripping the device tightly, she called out,

"My name is Jenny. Please state your name." The silence that followed pressed in on her, oppressive and unnatural. After a chilling moment, she tried again, her voice barely steady:

"Is anyone here, haunting this room, or are these stories just rumours?"

The silence seemed to deepen, as though something unseen was listening, waiting in the shadows. When she finally replayed the recording, the only sounds were her own nervous words and a faint hiss of static.

Suddenly, the static intensified, and a faint whisper emerged from the darkness—barely audible, but undeniably present: "I killed them…" Jenny's heart hammered in her chest. She froze, praying that her camera had picked up the voice as well. Was it her imagination, or was the room truly haunted?

A cold knot formed in her stomach as the impossibility of it sank in. She stood cautiously by the door, her heart rate increasing, while the chill in the air seemed to bite through her sweater, prickling her skin.

Jenny walked over to the bed and sat down, looking around the room, which was completely still and silent. She questioned whether she had truly heard those words on the recorder. After replaying the recording multiple times, she was certain of what she had heard. But as Jenny attempted to listen for any further sounds, the bathroom door began to open slowly. Its squealing hinges sounded unusually loud in the quiet room.

Startled, Jenny turned her attention toward the bathroom door. Standing from the bed, she asked, "Is this the spirit of the person who spoke on my recorder?" before cautiously approaching the bathroom.

The bathroom was shrouded in darkness until she flicked on the harsh overhead light, which buzzed and flickered before exposing a grimy bath beside a stained toilet and a cracked sink crowned with a tarnished mirror. The air was so thick with the stench of rot that every breath clawed at her throat, nearly making her retch.

Cold beads of condensation traced sinister patterns down the yellowing tiles. Jenny hesitated before peering behind the door. Nothing but a chipped, white table with deep gouges and stains on its surface. As her eyes darted anxiously around the room, her heart stuttered when she caught a glimpse in the mirror: standing directly behind her was a ghostly, hollow-eyed woman whose gaunt face twisted into a chilling half-smile. Paralysed by terror, Jenny stood helpless, uncertain what to do or say next.

Jenny quickly turned around, but found nothing there. When she glanced back at the mirror, her reflection stood alone—suddenly, the reflection smiled at her, though she herself had not. Startled, Jenny stumbled backward into the bathroom door as the reflection's smile grew unnaturally wide. Its lips began to crack and split like paper, blood running down in threads across the mirror.

Jenny moved quickly to the door, aware that she needed to leave. Her heart pounded in her chest as she glanced nervously over her shoulder, feeling a chill creep slowly up her spine.

There was an evil spirit present in the room—one that should never have been disturbed. Jenny felt certain that eyes were watching her from every dark corner. She rushed to the door and grabbed the key, but it was too hot to handle—the metal scorched her fingertips. She pulled her hand back quickly. She tried opening the window, but it wouldn't budge. The frame trembled under her hands, as if some unseen force held it shut. She then took out her phone from her pocket, but discovered it had been drained.

Jenny's thoughts raced as she contemplated how to escape the room.

Suddenly, a low voice behind her murmured,

"You will never leave alive. You will die here."

Startled, Jenny looked around but found the room empty. The atmosphere grew oppressive, as though the very walls were exhaling around her—not the building itself, but the walls alone, like lungs drawing breath. But when the bed creaked—without her moving—Jenny screamed in terror. From beneath the bed, two hands—gaunt, with yellowed nails and flayed skin—clawed at the carpet, pulling themselves from under the bed, fingers twitching.

Jenny stumbled from the bed, nearly tripping as she rushed to the door. She pounded on it with her fists, banging and screaming, but no one answered.

Behind her, the room seemed to grow darker and colder, and then a faint whisper came from the darkness:

"I drowned my children in the bath. They cried and cried until they died."

Jenny spun around. A woman was walking slowly towards her. The woman's dress was soaked, her hair hung down, unkempt and dirty, her eyes deep and hollow.

"I drowned them, and now I want you. Don't fight it, come with me, Jenny."

The door cracked beneath Jenny's feet. Water—black and thick—began seeping through the floorboards, rising to her ankles, then knees. Jenny wanted to move, but no matter how hard she tried, she was stuck. Small hands reached up at her, grabbing at her, slowly pulling her down.

When the concierge went to check the room the next morning, it was dry and spotless, with only Jenny's belongings left behind. The camera played on a loop—Jenny standing at the door, turning the key, and looking towards the window, smiling.

Some say that if you listen closely, you can still hear Jenny's voice crackling through the breeze that comes through the window of Room 7UN—though the room stands empty, and the Fisherman's Inn long abandoned, windows boarded against storm and sun.

Each year, on the anniversary, you can still hear Jenny banging on the door, her screams echoing down the hallway. There are new owners coming, with plans for the old inn, but will they be able to move the spirits on? The children who leave their handprints on the wallpaper, or the woman who killed her children—and Jenny. Will people want to stay there when they hear her screams?

From the road, passersby have sworn they've seen a pale figure coming out of the old inn, carrying bags, her hair streaming in a wind that doesn't blow. And every night, just before one o'clock in the morning, the mirror in Room 7UN fogs up. For a moment, a face forms in the condensation—wide-eyed, lips parted in an endless, silent scream. Then it vanishes, leaving only a cold drip trailing down the glass, like a tear that never dries.

Chapter 14
A Change of Scenery

Willow, I'll need you to drive us home tonight, as I've had a bit too much to drink," said Ashley, handing her the car keys.

"Slightly?" she responded with a laugh, accepting the keys. "I was planning to drive us home anyway." Willow then retrieved both her coat and Ashley's from the cloakroom attendant.

The typically ten-minute walk to the car park felt longer for Willow as she endeavoured to support Ashley, who staggered. The occasional flicker of streetlamps illuminated the path, casting long shadows on the pavement. Willow's arm was firmly around Ashley's waist, feeling his weight pressing down on her shoulder.

Upon reaching the car, Willow carefully assisted Ashley into the passenger seat. He slumped back, mumbling incoherently before closing his eyes. Willow stepped back, briefly stretching her sore back. She then reached into her bag, pulled out a cigarette, and lit it. The warm summer breeze carried the smoke upwards into the night sky, mingling with the distant hum of city life.

After finishing her cigarette, Willow crushed the butt under her shoe and entered the car. Ashley, with his head tilted forward, was gently snoring, his breath soft and rhythmic. Willow took a moment to look at him. Despite his dishevelled appearance, there was a calmness in his sleep.

The drive home from Richmond normally took thirty minutes, but tonight, the roads seemed unusually quiet. Willow glanced one more time at Ashley, smiled warmly at the peaceful look on his face, adjusted the rearview mirror, and then started the car. The engine purred softly to life.

About ten minutes into the journey home, a shadow appeared above the car, growing progressively darker. Willow became concerned, trying to keep her attention on the road while intermittently glancing towards the sky to identify the source of the shadow. The atmosphere grew tense, and an eerie silence enveloped the surroundings. Suddenly, the car jolted and then stopped, but the engine was still running. Willow's heart raced, and everything outside turned pitch black. There was no street lighting, no shops, no houses—just complete darkness. Her breath quickened as panic set in. She gripped the steering wheel tightly and looked over at Ashley, but he was still sound asleep. Shortly after, Willow lost consciousness, her mind drowning in fear and confusion.

Willow awoke suddenly in an unfamiliar room, her heart racing in her chest as she looked around the dimly lit space. She was dressed in a nightie that felt rough against her skin. Her eyes darted around the room: the walls were painted white, and there was a large cream-coloured wardrobe with round white handles. Next to it was a chest of drawers, the same colour as the wardrobe. There was a window on the opposite wall, with floral curtains. They didn't look right—there was something strange about this room.

There were no smells, like someone cooking breakfast or brewing fresh coffee. There were no sounds either: no traffic, no birds chirping, no children playing in the streets. Everything was still. Even the house was strangely silent. Beside her, Ashley was still asleep, snoring peacefully, as if he hadn't a care in the world. The strange thing was, Ashley was wearing pyjamas—something he never did. He always slept in the nude. The sight of him in pyjamas added to the weirdness of the situation.

Willow leaned over and gently shook Ashley, trying to suppress the rising panic within her.

"Ashley, wake up," she whispered, her voice trembling slightly.

Ashley mumbled incoherently, groaned, and slowly opened his eyes.

"What time is it?" he asked, rubbing his eyes and yawning deeply.

"I don't know," replied Willow, her brow furrowed in confusion.

"And more importantly, I don't know where we are or how we got here." She bit her lip, feeling a knot in her stomach as she reflected on the foggy events of the previous night. Vague images of the restaurant and walking to the car flickered in her mind, but everything else was a blur.

Ashley sat up, his eyes widening as he looked around the

unfamiliar room.

"Where the bloody hell are we?" he asked, looking at Willow.

He swung his legs over the side of the bed and stood up. The floor felt unusual beneath his bare feet—not like wood or tiles, but something resembling plastic. Then Ashley noticed what he was wearing.

"Who the hell dressed me for bed? What kind of joker put me in these pyjamas? More to the point, where did they come from? They're like wearing sandpaper. More importantly, where are our own clothes?" Ashley inquired as he examined the room.

Willow rose and walked to the wardrobe to check if their clothes had been put away. Upon opening it, she found it empty, and it felt like it was made of hard plastic. She approached the window and looked out. Everything was still—no breeze, no wind. The trees looked strange, almost false, and the grass appeared too green. Then she noticed there was no glass in the window, only plastic window frames. Willow turned to Ashley, who was now sitting on the edge of the bed, resting his head in his hands.

"This might be a challenging question for you, but can you remember anything from last night?" Willow asked, approaching him.

"What do you mean by 'a challenging question'? We had dinner with David and Sophie. They left, and then you and I went to the bar area and had a few more drinks. After that, I gave you the car keys, and we walked to the car," Ashley replied, appearing tired as he tried to recall their activities.

"Is that all you can remember? Well, I walked you to the car—or rather, we staggered to the car. I put you in the passenger seat, and you fell asleep. I had a cigarette, then started the car. About twenty minutes later, there was a large black shadow over the car, everything went black, and now I've woken up here, wherever this is," Willow explained, looking more confused now that she had said it out loud.

Ashley narrowed his eyes, trying to piece together any missing fragments.

"I'm sorry, but the whole thing is a blur," he mumbled as he got up from the bed and walked over to the door. He stopped, turned to Willow, and asked,

"Do you believe we were abducted by extraterrestrials?"

Willow blinked, surprised by the question.

"We were abducted, yes. By whom, I don't know. They've taken our clothes and my handbag, so we have no phones, and why on earth would they need to take our clothes? There are also some inconsistencies. Why is everything made of plastic? The window lacks glass, and everything outside appears strange. All I know is that we should leave immediately and find a way to contact the police." She grasped the door handle firmly.

The door opened without a sound, revealing a small hallway. Directly ahead was another closed door, and adjacent to it was a narrow staircase with steps covered in polished brown plastic designed to mimic wood. Listening intently, they detected no noise—only an unsettling stillness that caused their skin to tingle.

Proceeding cautiously down the stairs, they remained alert to any sounds. At the bottom of the stairs, to the left stood an archway, giving faint glimpses of kitchen furniture, while to the right, an open door exposed the lounge, its yellow walls barely visible in the darkness. In front of them was the front door, featuring a spyhole in its centre. Ashley swiftly grasped the handle, his heart pounding as if it were trying to escape his chest. With a determined twist, the door opened quietly and smoothly.

Upon stepping outside, they immediately noticed there were no cars or motorbikes, no streetlights, and the roads looked like they had never been used by any type of vehicle. The usual hum of daily life was eerily absent—no distant sound of motorway traffic, no children playing in a school playground, not even aircraft flying overhead. The pavement beneath their bare feet felt strange; it was smooth and not cold at all.

As they proceeded further down the road, they also noted the lack of birdsong. Not a single bird flew by or fed on the grass. The streets seemed deserted, and the houses stood silent and still, their windows dark like empty eyes watching them.

Ashley decided to approach one of the houses and knock on its door, leaving Willow by the gate. He walked up the stony path, trying to think of what to say to the person who might open the door. He paused at the door, heart pounding with trepidation, and glanced back at Willow, who gave him a reassuring nod to proceed. He knocked on the door three times, loudly. The sound reverberated through the quiet neighbourhood, but there was no response. The silence felt oppressive.

Determined not to give up, they tried knocking on several other doors. Each time, Ashley would stride up to the door, knock firmly, and wait, only to be met with the same eerie silence. The still air carried no hint of life or movement, and an unsettling feeling began to grow in their chests. Willow's eyes darted around nervously, while Ashley's frustration mounted with each unanswered door. They started to think they were alone in this ghostly, silent world.

"What's your assessment of our current situation?" Ashley inquired, sitting down on the curb of the road.

"I don't know what to say, if I'm being honest," Willow replied, sitting next to him. "I may have caused our death by crashing the car, and this is hell." Her voice trailed off, growing increasingly anxious as she pondered their predicament.

The eeriness of the empty streets was overwhelming, as if the village had been frozen in time. The shop windows displayed items that looked realistic at first glance, but upon closer inspection, the glossy finish of the plastic and the dullness of the clay gave away their true nature. The graveyard added to the unsettling atmosphere; the absence of inscriptions on the headstones hinted at stories untold and lives unrecorded.

They approached the church and pushed open the doors, only to find it was a mock-up constructed from bolstered wood and plaster brickwork. The stained-glass windows were merely pieces of coloured plastic on grey cardboard. The church bell, made of moulded foam, and the pews, bolstered wood painted to look old and worn, only added to the illusion.

"I think I know where we are," Willow said, beginning to smile as she looked around for cameras. "This appears to be a film set. It seems someone's playing a prank on us, and they've placed us in a film set."

Ashley looked around, more confused than ever. "Who would do such a thing to us?" He scanned the surroundings, hoping to see someone step out of the graveyard, laughing and saying 'got you,' but there was no one.

"Alright, you can come out now. The game's up," Willow said, walking toward the graveyard. "You may reveal yourself now, whoever you are," she added with a chuckle.

There was a moment of silence, and no one appeared, until a voice was heard from above.

"They have finally awakened," the voice said, seeming to originate from above.

Willow and Ashley looked up in astonishment as they saw two men, their heads and shoulders visible, both wearing glasses and white lab coats. The men were of considerable stature and were both staring down at them.

"Welcome to planet Marth," one of the men said. "There are different realms, and we brought you here from one of them. You are now our lab rats. Please enjoy your stay," he stated as he reached down to pick up Ashley and Willow.

If you and your spouse are planning a week-long holiday but cannot agree on a destination, ensure that your final choice leads to a comfortable and enjoyable experience. Avoid any situation where you end up as part of an experiment in a dollhouse, in a mock-up of an old English village, with giant researchers from another realm watching every move you make in their lab.

Chapter 15
Quiet Village

Michelle Boulder decided to take a short break—perhaps a few days, maybe a week—to get away from her dingy flat and the weight of her recent experiences with Lee and her dead-end job. She found herself overwhelmed by everything that had happened over the past two months. Her boyfriend, Lee, had ended their eight-year relationship, expressing a desire for new experiences and leaving her for someone younger by two years. The sudden end left Michelle grappling with feelings of abandonment and uncertainty about her future.

Michelle worked as a shelf stacker and cashier at Keane Supermarket, having started as a Saturday shelf stacker at seventeen and remaining in that role nine years later. Day after day, she went through the familiar routines at work, which had once provided her with a sense of belonging and stability but now seemed monotonous and isolating. Her interactions with customers were polite but distant; she often caught herself drifting into memories of happier times.

As an orphan, Michelle no longer had contact with her foster parents and lacked family support or advice. Without a close network or anyone to lean on, she struggled to process her emotions alone. The prospect of stepping away for a while felt necessary—a chance not only to escape her physical surroundings but also to clear her mind and perhaps rediscover some hope in the midst of change.

Michelle decided to drive to the coast for a few days. She planned it out on the map, trying to remember which route was best, but then decided to let the sat-nav guide her. She set it for Tastings, planning to spend a week there, which felt just right. She left late in the afternoon, a four-hour drive ahead, with the sat-nav estimating she'd arrive in Tastings around 7:34 pm. After driving for a while, Michelle started to feel hungry and somewhat tired, but she pressed on.

The road she was following was meant to lead to the coast. When she checked her sat-nav again, there was no signal. It was the third time the sat-nav had stopped working, and now the screen only showed a spinning wheel over a blank background. She pulled over onto a grassy verge to try and reset the device.

"Great, now my sat-nav has left me. Come on, work, will you?" she muttered as she turned it off and then on again. But it remained unresponsive. Looking up, she saw the narrow country lane lined with trees, the sun setting and night clouds rolling in. Michelle decided to continue driving, hoping to find a sign indicating the correct direction.

As Michelle travelled further, residential structures became increasingly infrequent, and the environment grew more untamed. The trees formed dense silhouettes against the sky, their leaves gently rustling in the breeze.

When Michelle checked her phone for reception, she realised it had died. She recalled the last time she ate, but couldn't remember exactly when. She looked around, but there were no villages or petrol stations nearby. Though fatigued, she remained attentive to the winding road ahead. Occasionally, small animals darted across her headlights before quickly retreating into the undergrowth.

The only disturbance to the tranquil environment was the sound of the engine and the crunch of tyres on gravel. Michelle tried to recall the directions she'd reviewed earlier as she navigated each bend, attentively searching for signposts that would confirm her route toward civilisation or indicate she was proceeding correctly.

With every passing mile, the edges of the narrow road seemed to dissolve into thick grass, and brambles crept closer, brushing against the car with a soft scratch. The cool air seeped through a barely open window, carrying the faint earthy scent of moss and wet soil from a recent rainfall. Occasionally, the moon broke through the clouds overhead, illuminating patches of the landscape and casting fleeting silver highlights on puddles scattered across the roadside.

As she gripped the steering wheel, Michelle's fingers occasionally tensed whenever the car jolted over a pothole or patches of loose stones. Her mind wandered to the maps she had studied back at home— fragmented images now, filled with doubts about missed junctions.

Each time her stomach rumbled, it reinforced her awareness of isolation. Not only was she alone, but no friendly lights offered reassurance in the distance—only darkness pressing in from all sides. Beneath the rhythmic drone of her vehicle, she caught faint, sporadic sounds—a distant cry from a fox. The journey felt suspended in time, each moment stretching longer as she strained to catch a glimpse of a signpost pointing her way back towards safety and human presence. After travelling several more miles, she noticed a hand-painted sign emerging ahead, partially concealed by the surrounding vegetation.

Welcome to Newton Moors, enjoy our lovely village and rest awhile.

Michelle arched an eyebrow in mild surprise. She did not recall encountering Newton Moors just outside Tastings on the maps. Nevertheless, with her phone now out of charge and the night creeping in, she determined that seeking accommodation in any available town or village was preferable to spending the night in her car.

The road led into the village square, lined with stone cottages and ivy-covered fences. The air had a faint scent of flowers and freshly cut grass. The area was eerily quiet, resembling a still image. Several people sat on benches outside a pub, chatting quietly. Michelle stopped her car and rolled down the window. The engine's hum faded into the perfect silence.

"I'm a bit lost. Is there any—uh—place I could use a phone?"

An old man replied, his grey hair poking out from under a flat cap. His weathered hands rested on a cane. "No phones here. No need for that stuff. Newton Moors is a place for quiet living and relaxation."

A woman next to him, wrapped in a faded tartan shawl, said, "You should stay for a while. You seem tired." Her face was kind but inscrutable, her bright eyes studying Michelle closely.

Michelle responded with a polite laugh, though she felt uneasy about their invitation. Her fingers drummed nervously on the steering wheel, and she glanced down at the sat-nav.

The friendliness of the couple felt genuine, yet something in their unwavering gazes left her feeling exposed and uncertain in this timeless place.

She spent the night at a bed-and-breakfast, where the accommodations were exemplary—a comfortable bed and a notably cosy atmosphere. The bed-and-breakfast was immaculately maintained, to an almost impeccable degree. Every surface gleamed without a trace of dust, and even the linens smelled faintly of lavender.

What Michelle found strange, however, was that there were no clocks, televisions, radios, or mirrors. The absence lent the room an unusual sense of timelessness and introspection. Ambient light from antique brass lamps created gentle shadows that danced across the contemporary patterned wallpaper, encouraging relaxation and quiet contemplation.

Upon inquiring about these omissions, the host, a young man named Dougie, responded only with a polite smile, his eyes warm but revealing nothing. It was as though he enjoyed keeping the air of mystery intact.

"No need for timepieces here. We live by the light of the sun, and we go to bed when the moon is at its highest," Dougie replied with a smile.

Michelle decided to take a walk through the village, where she observed an elderly couple engaged in gardening. The man was carefully trimming the rose bushes, while the woman knelt beside him, pulling weeds from the soft earth. Their trowels clinked faintly with each motion. A teenage girl was sweeping the porch and paused to greet Michelle with a wave. Upon noticing her, she rested her broom against the wall of the cottage and offered a bright, friendly smile.

Nearby, children were playing hopscotch in silence, their chalk-drawn squares faded against the dusty stone pavement. Their concentration was clear in their furrowed brows as they hopped lightly from one square to the next. Each of them acknowledged Michelle as she passed, their smiles composed and reserved, offering brief nods and glances that spoke to the quiet warmth of the community. The air carried the subtle scent of fresh soil and blooming lilacs, accompanied by the warm sunshine.

That night, Michelle had a vivid dream. Her headlights cut through sheets of rain, casting warped reflections on the wet asphalt. Suddenly, a figure darted across the road in front of her car, its outline blurred by the downpour. Then, there were shards of glass shattering in slow motion, followed by the twisted groan of metal as it crumpled. In the midst of the chaos, she heard a distant voice—soft at first, then rising urgently, calling her name over the roar of the storm.

She awoke abruptly, gasping for breath, beads of sweat clinging to her forehead, dampening her hair. Her bedding was tangled and half-draped over the edge of the bed, as if she had thrashed in her sleep, still haunted by the echoes of her nightmare.

She picked up her phone from the bedside cabinet, but it still hadn't charged, despite being left plugged in overnight. Frustrated, she checked the cable, jiggled the charger in the socket, and pressed the power button again, but nothing happened. She let out a small sigh, wondering if the phone was completely dead or just needed a new cable.

Sitting up in bed, she looked around the room. Sunlight was entering through the curtains, casting golden lines across the room and warming the wooden floor. She took a shower, got dressed, and made her way to the kitchen. After pouring herself a glass of water, she stepped outside, walking into the morning mist. The village was already alive with activity—people gardening, tending to rhododendrons and hanging baskets, or hanging up laundry that remained damp, sagging on the clotheslines. Children were chasing each other across the square and down the lanes, while three boys played marbles over a drain cover.

Michelle approached Dougie, who was busy piling firewood next to his cottage, and asked, "Is there somewhere nearby I can get some petrol? I think I should be leaving soon. I don't want to overstay my welcome." Her voice carried a hint of regret as she glanced around at the cosy little village and all the friendly faces.

Dougie wiped his hands on his trousers, then stared at her almost sympathetically. "You can try the road you came in on, but I don't think you'll get far."

Michelle looked at him with a puzzled expression. As she looked around the village, she suddenly became aware of the profound silence. No birds were singing, no wind, and absent were the sounds of children playing—no giggles, no footsteps—only complete stillness.

Her confusion deepened as she strained to listen, trying to detect even the faintest rustle of leaves or distant city sounds. The air now felt unusually still, almost heavy, pressing against her skin with a faint chill.

Shadows stretched long across the ground, unmoving in the stagnant air. She glanced over at the empty park benches and the two swings that hung motionless, their chains perfectly still.

A cold unease settled in Michelle's chest, but she forced a smile. "I guess I'll see how far I can get, then," she replied, masking her uncertainty. She thanked Dougie quietly and returned to her room, gathering her few belongings. She took one last look around the room, lingering on the empty spaces where clocks or mirrors might have hung— a strange absence that now seemed more ominous than charming. Her unease deepened as she realised how quiet the village felt this morning. There were no cars, only hers, no barking dogs, no distant hum of traffic.

She stepped out to her car. The engine turned over reluctantly before catching. As she drove out of the village, passing faces that smiled and nodded at her departure, Michelle found her mind wandering back to her dream. The memory of shattered glass and the spectral figure sent a chill down her spine. She pushed the thought aside, focusing on the narrow road as it twisted through the country lanes.

The trees seemed to lean closer, forming a tunnel of green and shadow. Michelle tried to follow the route she had taken to get to the village, searching for signs of another town or any sign of life beyond Newton Moors. The deeper she drove, the thicker the woods became, with branches scraping the car roof like fingers trying to pull her back. She kept glancing down at her useless sat-nav, wishing she could get it to work—anything to break the spell of isolation.

She passed a fox darting across the road, its coat gleaming momentarily in a shaft of sunlight. The road dipped, rose, and twisted until the scenery grew unfamiliar, then strangely repetitive. Michelle's foot eased off the accelerator as a sense of déjà vu crept over her—the same mossy fallen tree, the same broken wooden gate. She frowned and pressed onward, telling herself it was just her nerves.

But then, the unmistakable shape of the hand-painted sign appeared again:

Welcome to Newton Moors, enjoy our lovely village and stay awhile.

She brought the car to an abrupt stop, astonished to find herself once again at the village. The landscape was eerily familiar—narrow lanes lined with ancient stone cottages, fields stretching into the mist. The villagers were assembled, neither angry nor surprised. Instead, they greeted her with smiles and waves.

Michelle exited the car, her hands trembling as she grasped the car door. An elderly lady approached her, welcoming her back. Her silver hair was neatly braided, and kindness radiated from her gentle eyes.

"I wish to leave. I want to return home. Please, allow me to leave," Michelle stated, tears streaming down her face, her voice quivering with desperation.

The elderly lady reached out, resting a comforting hand on Michelle's shoulder, while others gathered closer, murmuring words of reassurance.

"You already did," the elderly lady said gently, her voice soothing but heavy with meaning. "Long ago, but you didn't listen."

Michelle's hands shook, and through her tears, she looked at the elderly lady, bewildered. "What do you mean, I didn't listen?"

The crowd parted, and the elderly lady pointed towards the church. Michelle's eyes followed her gesture. There, standing in the shadow of the church, was a figure. A woman, her clothing ripped and dirty, soaked with blood. As the figure turned, Michelle's heart dropped— the face of the woman was her own.

Michelle backed away in horror. "But how?" she mumbled, shaking her head. "That's not real, that's not…"

The doppelgänger stared at her, eyes wide and glassy, and then it spoke, its voice hauntingly familiar. "You did this. You did this to yourself. You fell asleep."

Michelle's last memory resurfaced, cold and clear, like a dead fish washing ashore—a rain-slick road, empty and desolate. She felt tired and hungry. She had fallen asleep behind the wheel, and then she was jolted awake by the fox running across the road. The crash, the scream—it was hers. The scream was real, not a dream.

She had been in Newton Moors ever since.

"You died, Michelle," Dougie said softly, his voice breaking the silence. "We are all dead. Newton Moors is where the forgotten come. The ones who never realised they were gone, who passed over."

Michelle sank to her knees, trying to make sense of the revelation. "This isn't fair. I didn't know…"

"I know," Dougie replied, his voice kind but firm. "And now we are all residents of Newton Moors."

The villagers gathered around her, some crying, others laughing softly, but all of them stuck, trapped in the same eerie stillness.

"You'll forget again," the elderly lady said gently, her voice soothing yet filled with a melancholic certainty. "In time. We all do."

"That's how we stay," she added softly.

And as Michelle looked around the village—the perfect, silent place—she realised, with growing dread, that she was already forgetting.

Chapter 16
Marionette

At the outskirts of town, where most retail stores are either vacant, boarded up, or repurposed as charity shops, stands an old toy shop that now sees few visitors due to the prevalence of internet shopping. The owner, Mr. Farley, who never seems to age, has run the shop for decades and has witnessed many changes over the years.

The shop's facade is faded, with its once-bright sign now cracked and peeling. The wooden door, with its brass handle, is dulled by decades of use. Through the display window, only shadowy glimpses of the interior can be seen—stacked board games and model kits, all yellowed with time.

Inside, the space is densely packed, with shelves burdened by dusty dolls, action figures, clockwork animals, and boxes of train sets. A subtle aroma of cedar and aged varnish permeates the air. Occasionally, delicate music from a wind-up music box filters through the shop, mingling with the faint ticking of the shop clock mounted on the wall above the counter. The dim lighting comes from only two of the four fluorescent tubes that still work.

High on a shelf behind the counter, a marionette named Zicardo is displayed. Characterised by its elongated limbs, dark wooden face, and faded red tunic with black trousers, Zicardo's porcelain eyes are notably lifelike. The marionette is encased behind a locked glass display cabinet. Shadows play across its features, giving it a canny presence even when still. The craftsmanship is evident in the marionette's slender, intricately carved fingers and the delicately painted designs on its small black boots.

Mr. Farley insists that Zicardo originates from a Spanish puppet troupe and was acquired during his travels many decades ago. The tale is accompanied by sepia photographs pinned to the wall beside Zicardo—images of masked performers beneath striped tents, and a young Mr. Farley shaking hands with an elderly puppeteer beneath strings of lanterns. Zicardo's cabinet is secured by a lock, with the key always kept on a silver chain worn by Mr. Farley. The glass panel of the cabinet is etched with curling motifs and tiny stars in the corners.

Local rumours suggest that, on certain nights, movements can be seen within the case or faint sounds, resembling strings being plucked, may be heard, though these claims remain unverified. Some people whisper about flickering lights seen at strange hours or swear they have glimpsed Zicardo's head turning, but these stories linger in the minds of those who visit, adding to the mysterious allure of the already peculiar shop.

Danny Larver is a seventeen-year-old known for frequently accepting challenges. For example, he once jumped from a bridge onto a moving train after being offered a mere two hundred pounds as a bet. On another occasion, his friends locked him in an old hospital ward overnight, because it was rumoured to be haunted, and he accepted the challenge to stay alone.

Danny has developed a reputation among his friends for never backing down from a dare, no matter how risky or bizarre. The adrenaline rush and the sense of accomplishment drive him to push his limits.

During the bridge jump, the wind whipped against his face as he leapt, his heart pounding wildly, but he landed safely on the train, earning cheers and gasps of disbelief. When confined in the abandoned hospital, the eerie silence and echoing footsteps sent chills down his spine, yet he stayed put until sunrise, proving his bravery.

So, when Craig suggested spending a few hours alone in the old toy shop one night while Mr. Farley slept upstairs in the flat above, Danny grinned, eager to prove that no challenge was too daunting for him.

"Simply enter through the back window and remain in the shop for a few hours," Craig advised Danny, giving him a reassuring pat on the back. "It's that straightforward," he added with a light chuckle.

"To make it more interesting, why not take a photo of Zicardo?" Josh suggested, glancing at the others and sharing an amused smile, the kind reminiscent of a child on Christmas Eve.

"That scary thing?" Craig said, his voice tinged with a noticeable tremor. "I've heard old Farley talks to it like it's his own child."

"I heard someone say it moves when you're not looking," Mandy added, drawing closer to Josh for reassurance.

"Let's set aside the scary stories," Danny remarked with a laugh. "It's just a puppet, made of wood, simple as that. Honestly, I'm more concerned about the type of spiders that might be inside," he added as he checked his torch to make sure it was working properly.

The group made their way to the rear of the shop and gathered at the storeroom window. Craig glanced at his watch. "It's six minutes past midnight. If you stay inside for about four to five hours, we'll wait here for you," he said, smiling before helping Danny up to the window.

"A solid four hours at least," Josh whispered. "Watch out for those killer spiders," he added with a chuckle, as Danny disappeared through the window.

The air inside the storeroom was denser than Danny had anticipated, as if it had retained the quiet of the years. Shelves displayed rows of old toys, covered with dust and cobwebs—porcelain dolls with fixed expressions, tin wind-up monkeys missing their keys, and stacks of electric train sets waiting to be played with.

The musty scent of paper and damp wood mingled with a faint metallic tang, lingering in every breath. Danny heard his friends chatting and laughing outside as he moved from the storeroom into the main shop. The counter ahead held an old-fashioned till, and next to it was a folded newspaper with a half-completed crossword puzzle. Beneath the counter were several paper bags bearing the shop's name and a plate with an empty crisp packet.

The streetlights coming through the main shop window cast long shadows on the walls and floor, dappling the space with patterns that seemed to shift with every movement Danny made. He walked among the shelves of toys and games, the uneven floorboards creaking underfoot. Each step stirred up tiny motes of dust that floated lazily through the still air.

Near the entrance was a white metal basket full of footballs, a spider's web stretching across them, glistening slightly in the slanted light.

"I knew there would be spiders in here somewhere," Danny mumbled, shivering at the thought of the unseen creatures.

He then directed his torch toward the counter. The light reflected off Zicardo, a marionette displayed inside a tall glass cabinet. To Danny, it seemed larger than any marionette he had seen before, with long, thin limbs, a fixed grin, red cheeks, and wide black eyes that appeared to reflect light from every angle. The puppet's paint was chipped along the jaw and its hands, but the meticulous detail of its costume—tiny brass buttons, faded black velvet trousers—hinted at better days.

For a moment, Danny wondered if those glossy eyes were following his every move. The silence seemed to press in even closer.

"You are decidedly unsettling," Danny muttered quietly to himself, pulling out his phone and snapping a photo.

As Danny continued to look around, his footsteps echoed softly on the wooden floor. Suddenly, he heard the creak of a door somewhere in the dark, followed by a faint and rhythmic tapping, reminiscent of fingers drumming methodically on a wooden surface. A shiver crawled up his spine. He swiftly turned around, aiming his torch toward the cluttered counter. The cone of light trembled in his hand, but there was nothing visible except dust motes dancing in its beam.

"Craig, is that you?" Danny whispered, scanning each shadowy aisle and shelf with mounting vigilance. His pulse pounded louder in his ears, and the silence seemed to press in around him.

When his torch illuminated Zicardo again, he noticed the glass display case remained tightly shut. Still, an indistinct shift in the atmosphere—perhaps a sudden draft or a change in the air's heaviness—suggested that something or someone might be watching him from one of the many shadows, waiting to pounce at any moment.

"Take a deep breath and carry on. It's just an old toy shop; there's nothing here that can harm you," Danny reassured himself, though his heart pounded relentlessly, and every flicker of movement in his periphery seemed potentially threatening.

Danny investigated both the storeroom and the main shop before settling onto a stool near the counter, attentively noting the passing traffic outside and the subtle creaks within the premises.

The faded gold lettering on the window reflected dim streetlights, and boxes were stacked haphazardly along the walls, casting jagged shadows that shifted each time a car drove by.

Checking his phone, he saw that it was **2:27 a.m.** "A few more hours," he murmured, his voice muffled by the silence. Danny methodically inspected the shop, the cool beam of his torch sweeping over dusty shelves and stacks of neglected board games. He stood up, stretched, and began walking around the shop again. His footsteps echoed softly as he made his way past rows of action figures and dolls.

Suddenly, Danny's eyes widened with concern—Zicardo's glass display door was open and the puppet was no longer there.

Danny stepped back, his heart racing. He methodically swept his torch across every dark corner. Shadows flickered along the walls, and the faint scent of dust and mould filled the air, intensifying his unease.

In a whisper, he asked, "Who's there? Who moved the puppet?" Each word echoed in the silence, swallowed quickly by the oppressive darkness.

Feeling increasingly uneasy, Danny advanced towards the storeroom, his steps slow and cautious as the floorboards creaked beneath him. He then heard footsteps ahead—neither heavy nor hurried, but slow and deliberate, as if someone was attempting to approach unnoticed. The sound seemed to come from just beyond a row of battered wooden shelving, where figures of clowns stared blankly into nothingness.

He directed his torch towards the source of the sound, but whatever moved behind the shelving did so too quickly to be identified, though its shape appeared unmistakably human.

A chill ran down his spine as he caught a brief flash of a pale hand disappearing behind a stack of boxes. He gripped the torch tighter, scanning the shadows for another glimpse.

As he moved towards the window, thin white threads began to descend from above. Each strand fell steadily, resembling spider silk. He tried to leave, but the threads seemed to wrap around his wrists, arms, legs, and ankles of their own accord. The threads tightened incrementally, pulling him back into the shop. He tried to scream out to his friends, but the threads tightened around his throat, choking off his words.

Danny woke up with a jolt. The attic was poorly lit, with only a single light bulb hanging down in front of him. It smelled musty, and the air felt damp. Danny realised he was in intense pain—his legs and arms ached terribly. As he looked down at his legs and then across to his arms, he saw the horrifying truth: he was suspended from the ceiling beams of the attic, the threads piercing through his arms, hands, legs, and feet, like a marionette.

Danny attempted to wriggle free, but it was futile. Desperately looking around for something to assist him in escaping, he could only see numerous old curtains scattered across the floor, a few broken carved chairs lying on their sides, and stacks of yellowed newspapers and magazines piled haphazardly around him.

Glancing upwards, Danny's eyes widened in horror. Hundreds of strings extended from his limbs, stretching towards the rafters above and vanishing into the oppressive darkness. It was clear now that each slight movement he made was not his own doing. An external force appeared to control him. The floorboards groaned from somewhere in the shadows, and then came the unmistakable sound of laughter.

Zicardo emerged from the dark, his wooden face devoid of any visible strings or external guidance. His head was slightly tilted to one side, and his dark eyes reflected the faint light in a chilling manner. He moved with an unnerving smoothness, each step deliberate and unhurried, as if he were fully aware of Danny's growing panic.

Zicardo approached, his voice a whisper, "You shouldn't have come here. But I'm glad you did," he added with a giggle that echoed eerily through the attic.

"Come forward, Mr. Farley," Zicardo demanded, turning his head towards the shadows.

From the darkness emerged Mr. Farley, his face shadowed, his movements slow and deliberate as he approached Danny.

"Zicardo is always looking for new toys to play with, you see," Mr. Farley murmured softly, a twisted smile pulling at his lips. "I give him new toys, and he keeps me alive. You're already prepared to be the new marionette. All we need to do now is shrink you down to size."

Danny's attempt to scream was cut off as the threads around his throat tightened. Panic surged through him, but the more he struggled, the tighter they became. "You'll learn to enjoy being a marionette, Danny," Mr. Farley continued, his voice oddly calm. "Give it time. The pain fades once you stop trying to move on your own."

Zicardo raised his hand, and Danny's body obeyed. He found himself dancing, his limbs moving as though they had a will of their own. The more he danced, the more Zicardo giggled in delight, his wooden face twisting into an expression of glee.

"My sweet marionette made of flesh," Zicardo purred. "How beautiful you dance."

Mr. Farley watched the scene, nodding in approval. "I'll leave you to have your fun, Zicardo," he said with a sigh. "But please, make this one last a bit longer than the others."

With that, he turned and walked away, leaving Danny to move in a macabre dance, controlled by forces beyond his understanding.

Strangely enough, Danny was never found. His friends were questioned by the police, and his parents made several televised appeals, hoping for any information. The police even questioned Mr. Farley at his shop and conducted a thorough search of the premises, but no evidence was uncovered.

Meanwhile, Zicardo gained a new companion in his display case: a marionette boy dressed in a dark blue hoodie, black jeans, and black trainers. His glassy blue eyes and strings that seemed to lead to nowhere made him unsettlingly lifelike. On occasion, late at night, those watching the puppets might notice them moving—smooth and deliberate, unlike the erratic movements of common toys. And there were times when one of them appeared to shed a tear.

After Danny's disappearance, tension in the town grew thick. Whispers filled the narrow streets, and neighbours eyed each other with suspicion. The televised appeals by Danny's distraught parents brought the community together for vigils, but as the days passed without any news, hope began to fade. During this time, Mr. Farley's shop became a point of local fascination. People claimed the air inside felt colder than before, and some swore they heard faint, muffled sobs coming from the shop close to closing time.

Danny, nestled among the older puppets, often drew long, curious stares. The marionette boy, with his eerily lifelike features—his hair meticulously painted, his clothing style almost too realistic, and his hands hanging limply by his sides—stood apart from the others. His vacant stare seemed to follow visitors across the shop, and at times, a faint glint of moisture could be seen at the corner of one glassy eye.

Those who had stayed until closing time insisted that the gentle sway of the new puppet's body couldn't be explained by drafts alone. It was as if the marionette responded to something unseen, perhaps even mourning silently, its tears hidden from all but the most observant. Some claimed the air around it grew heavier, colder, as if the very presence of the marionette invited a deeper, unspoken sorrow.

Chapter 17
The Room with no Shadows

The conference room was windowless, its walls coated in a dull, institutional beige that seemed to swallow light rather than reflect it. The air carried the faint, metallic scent of recycled ventilation, as if the air had been breathed a million times before.

Above, a slender band of coloured tubing murmured softly, its light flickering in a rhythm—each flicker slightly longer than the last, like an irregular heartbeat. The brief flashes cast deep shadows across the corners where walls and ceiling met, twisting the space into grotesque, fleeting shapes.

In the centre of the room stood a wooden table, its surface polished to a clinical sheen beneath the flickering light. A faint circular gouge marred the tabletop, a relic from many cups of coffee set down absentmindedly during long hours of waiting. The light reflected off the table in shallow, distorted blurs—casting away the warmth, revealing the room's inherent fatigue.

Six wooden chairs, each upholstered in maroon fabric faded to the colour of bureaucracy, were arranged in a perfect circle around the table. Their alignment was unnerving—far too precise, as if governed by an invisible hand. The fabric of the seats bore faint impressions, where previous occupants had sat too long, their weight pressing down upon the once-pliant cushions, now resigned.

The wooden floor, polished but mottled, was streaked with black scuff marks and ghostly patterns of shoe prints—each one left behind like forgotten echoes of those who had passed through.

Even the silence in the room felt like a texture, thick and patient, lingering just beyond the hum of the overhead lights. It waited—polite, yet insistent.

One by one, they arrived, precisely on time, each to the minute.

The first, a pale, nervous man in an ill-fitting blazer, checked his phone three times before entering, as if expecting a last-minute reprieve.

The second, a sharply dressed woman, clutching her handbag tightly to her chest, scanned the room and frowned at the absence of windows.

The third and fourth exchanged awkward nods, recognising each other from past business dealings.

The fifth arrived late, by less than a minute, but looked as though he had sprinted the last stretch.

Each had received the same cryptic email, signed only "Your Adviser," promising a confidential lecture to unlock their true professional potential. None of them could recall who had authorised it.

The woman giving the lecture was already waiting. She sat perfectly straight in one of the chairs, her charcoal-grey suit immaculate, her posture a study in control. Her hair, dark as the night, was pulled back into a knot so tight that it seemed to pull the corners of her face upward. Her eyes were darker still—so dark it was impossible to distinguish her pupils from the surrounding iris.

She rose without haste, moving toward the table.

"Please," she said, motioning to the chairs. Her voice was low and deliberate, threaded with an uncanny resonance, as though it didn't emerge from her throat but from somewhere much deeper, much older. "You're right on time."

No one asked how she already knew their names. She spoke them softly, almost reverently—as if reciting something remembered rather than learned.

As they took their seats, the faint hum of the overhead lights deepened into a tone that pressed against the walls, settling behind their eyes. Without a hand touching it, the door eased shut with a slow, final click.

The woman watched them in silence for a moment, her eyes unreadable, before drawing her chair closer to the table. The sound of its legs scraping the floor seemed to stretch, thin and sharp. She folded her hands neatly before her and smiled—a small, deliberate curve of the lips that never reached her eyes.

"Before we begin," she said, her voice smooth as glass, "I want to thank each of you for agreeing to this lecture. By the time we're finished, you'll understand why you were chosen. So please, make yourselves comfortable. You're here to unburden yourselves. Only truth can make you stronger."

The air thickened, heavy with something invisible but insistent. Her voice, when she spoke again, carried a subtle pulse beneath the words—a rhythm that crept beneath the skin. At first, they resisted. But the lilt of her voice—warm, cajoling, impossibly soft—began to press against the fragile walls of their minds. It slipped through the cracks, and within seconds, they wavered, melting away like sugar in a cup of hot water.

Her questions were soft and precise, slipping through their defenses as if she already knew the answers. Weaknesses, betrayals, private failures whispered into the stale air, one after another, each confession more desperate than the last. Through it all, she only smiled, listening—like someone harvesting something invisible, something they could not see.

The father who had abandoned his sick child in the hospital waiting room, because he was late meeting a secret lover. The mother who had secretly resented her child's success. The betrayal of a colleague's trust for a promotion.

Each confession deepened the silence, until it was no longer a space but a weight, pressing them deeper into their chairs.

The young woman, who had laughed and joked at her friend's

tragedy to make herself feel superior.

The quiet man, who had stolen years of wages from his dying employer.

The brash one, who humiliated others simply out of fear of being forgotten.

And the last, who turned away each time cruelty unfolded near her.

Their voices cracked as they spoke. Some wept, others laughed nervously, and some stared down at their own trembling hands, the weight of their confessions pressing down on them.

The adviser listened patiently, never judging, never interrupting. Only when the lecture had finished did she smile—a thin, sad smile, as though pitying them all. As the adviser slowly stood, she pushed the chair back with the back of her legs, causing it to scrape faintly against the wooden floor. She glanced around the table, meeting each pair of eyes with a calm, measured smile, before offering her thanks for their attendance.

For a moment, no one moved. Then, as if a spell had broken, they all stirred at once—blinking, stretching, and glancing at one another in mild confusion, as though waking from a deep and private dream.

They had forgotten what exactly had been said—only that they had spoken, freely, even intimately. It felt as though they had laid themselves bare before the others, though none could recall the words they had used or the reasons why. Yet a curious lightness filled them, an inward buoyancy. The air in the room seemed thinner, easier to breathe.

A low hum of conversation began to fill the space as they rose from their seats. Someone laughed quietly; another clapped a colleague on the shoulder. They exchanged pleasantries about the "lecture," agreeing on how enlightening it had been. The phrases *self-discipline, focus, and motivation* came up again and again, as if those had been the cornerstones of what they had learned. Their memories, like shuffled cards, rearranged themselves neatly into this new pattern.

One by one, they shook the adviser's hand. Her grip was cool and deliberate. Her eyes followed each of them as they turned toward the door, smiling faintly as if she knew something they did not.

Then, as the last of them stepped across the threshold into the corridor, he was there.

A tall man stood in the corridor, waiting as though he had always been meant to. His black suit absorbed the faint light, its surface dull and depthless. His tie resembled the colour of dried blood. His face was narrow, almost elegant in its severity—pale, drawn tight over sharp bones. No expression stirred it. But his eyes—his eyes were endless. They had no colour that could be named, only a cold, dark expanse that seemed to pull at the edges of thought itself.

He inclined his head slightly as the group emerged, and one by one, their smiles faltered.

No one could say why.

The tall man stepped slowly forward. His shoes seemed to glide silently across the floor. His eyes, cold and fathomless, swept across their faces.

"You misunderstood," he rasped, his voice like gravel crushed beneath iron. "This was no lecture. This was a snare that drew you here. Each of you has sinned—done something foul—and justice has slept too long. None of you were ever punished..."

He paused, the silence bending around his words. "Until now."

The air thickened, pressing against their lungs.

"You have all spoken your truths," he continued, the lights flickering with each word. "And truth binds. Judgment has already been rendered. I have weighed you all... and for what you've done, I can pronounce only one sentence."

His head tilted slightly, the faintest, dreadful smile curling at the edge of his mouth.

"Death."

A tremor ran through the room. The floor groaned beneath them, and the table and chairs rattled violently. A scream tore through the air, followed by frantic prayers.

As they stumbled backwards, the door slammed shut with a

violent crack, the echo swallowing their cries. The lights flared blindingly bright, buzzing, then flickering—once, twice—before steadying into a sickly, colourless glow.

And then came the silence.

They turned to one another—and froze.

The light was still there, but something was wrong. It didn't fall anymore; it hovered, source-less, flat.

Their bodies stood stark and pale beneath it, but the floor beneath them was clean, empty.

"No shadows, there are no shadows, not one," said one of the women, her voice high with panic.

Then the tall man spoke again, softly, almost with a hint of pity. "You see?" he said. "The light no longer belongs to you."

The adviser—still seated, still calm—folded her hands and inclined her head slightly, as if the formalities were over.

The tall man stepped forward and gave a smirk as he looked at them. "You confessed. That was the bargain. Now your deeds will return to you."

He turned to the first:

The father who had abandoned his sick child for a night of passion with his lover. The man froze and bowed his head. The rattle of a cough emerged from somewhere in the shadows—soft at first, then harsh and ragged, a deathbed appeal pulled through time in an empty hospital room. His breath came short, the air thick with the sour tang of sickness. He clutched his chest, not from pain, but from the sudden crushing weight pressed against him.

Something warm and fever-hot writhed in his arms. He dared to look down. A small boy lay cradled against him, so light, so fragile, his skin slick with sweat and fever burns. Wide eyes, glassy and hollow, peered into his eyes that were once bright, now filmed over with betrayal. The child's lips parted, trembling with effort, and through them slipped a single word: "Father." The syllable cracked him open like a hammer to an egg.

He staggered backwards, shaking his head, but the child did not let go. His breath rattled, then slowed, then stilled—before the small body began to crumble. Fingers, arms, face—all flaking into blackened ash, disintegrating in his grasp. He tried to let go, but the child's hands clung to him, even as they collapsed into nothing.

Then the ash swirled and turned against him.

It swirled upward, a storm of grey filling his mouth, his nose, and his eyes. He gagged, choking, clawing at his throat as dust poured inside him, thick and bitter with the taste of fever and betrayal. He stumbled, dropped to his knees, his chest convulsing. He tried to scream, but the sound was buried—smothered beneath the choking tide of what he had deserted.

And as he fell, suffocating on the dust of his own guilt, he heard it again—the soft, rasping cough, closer now, whispering from inside his lungs.

The second: the young woman who had rejoiced at her friend's misery. Her reflection shimmered in the polished surface of the table, a perfect likeness—until it smiled. She wasn't smiling. Yet the image below grinned broadly, its teeth gleaming like tiny shards of light. The reflection leaned closer, though she had not moved, and whispered words she could not hear but somehow understood: *I know what you are.*

The laughter that followed was not a sound, but a sensation—cold fingers brushing along her spine. The reflection began to change, its features softening and warping, showing her friend's face instead—tear-streaked, pleading, betrayed. The young woman recoiled, her heart hammering.

"No… it wasn't like that," she whispered, but the reflection only tilted its head and smiled wider, its eyes empty and shining with liquid sorrow.

The surface of the table rippled like ink. Shadows coiled within its depths, forming shapes that resembled reaching hands, grasping mouths—mirroring the very pain she had delighted in. Her own reflection began to dissolve into the darkness, until what looked back at her was no longer human—a figure woven from guilt and enjoyment, its grin splitting from ear to ear in cruel celebration.

"Do you see now?" it seemed to whisper. "Joy is a blade that cuts both ways."

Then the table opened like a wound. Her reflection's arms reached upward, not to seize her, but to embrace her, pulling her down gently, inexorably, into the shining blackness.

Her screams never came. She only gasped once, as though falling into freeing water—and was gone.

The surface smoothed over, gleaming once more. In its depths, a faint echo of laughter lingered, soft and sorrowful, as though the table itself mourned what it had devoured.

The third: the quiet thief who thought he was clever. Silent hands, darting eyes, never caught, never questioned. But this afternoon, as he slipped the coins into his sleeves, something shifted. The weight grew heavier, pulling his arms downward until his bones ached. Then came the sound—an endless chime, a ringing that grew louder, echoing throughout the room.

Coins began spilling from his sleeves, clinking to the floor, but they did not scatter and rest. They multiplied, tumbling over one another— a gleaming torrent that spread like spilt blood. His eyes widened. He clawed at them, shoving the coins back into his sleeves, but each coin scored his skin, branding his flesh with perfect round blisters. His palms blackened, cracked, split open as smoke rose from the wounds. Still, the river of coins rose. It reached his ankles, burning through his shoes, peeling skin from the bone. He tried to stagger forward, but every step sank him deeper into molten flood. Coins wormed into his trousers, his shirt, sliding like insects against his skin, burrowing into the wounds they had made.

The coins climbed higher, sloshing against his chest, pressing their weight into his ribs until he could barely draw breath. It was no longer cool, solid metal—each coin dripped like hot wax, boiling, bubbling, clinging. He thrashed, screaming, but the sound was muted as the coins slithered between his lips, filling his mouth, searing his tongue to cinders. He gagged, but more coins forced their way down his throat, spilling molten trails through his body, blistering him from within.

His nostrils flared, desperate for air, and the river seized the chance—pouring inside, drowning him not with water, but with liquid fire. His vision was reduced to black and gold. His last scream rose as nothing more than a hiss, the shriek of flesh melting impossible weight beneath.

The river did not stop. When it was finished with him, nothing remained but a blackened husk, jaw frozen open in a silent scream. The coins continued spilling, piling higher, eager for another thief to taste their curse.

The fourth man, very brash, took a couple of steps back when the tall man looked at him. He smiled at him, then let out a nervous laugh that cut through the silence of the room. He basked in everyone's discomfort as though it were keeping him alive.

But when his laughter died, the room did not return to silence. Instead, a faint whisper rose—thin and papery, like dry leaves rubbing together. It came from nowhere but everywhere at once. He faltered. He looked around. The adviser watched warily, uncertain, as the whisper began to form words: "Do you remember me?"

He blinked, his throat tightening. He stumbled toward the table. On the polished surface, his reflection stared back, but it was wrong—too vivid, too solid. It smiled with a cruel awareness, mocking him as he had mocked so many others.

Then the reflection began to fade—not vanish, but erode, as if memory itself were being scraped away. His reflection's face grew indistinct, smudged, dissolving into the dark sheen of the table until there was nothing.

He gasped and found that the whisper was now inside his mind, peeling back his thoughts. He tried to speak, to make some biting remark that might reassert him, but no words came. His voice caught in his throat, trapped there like a dying moth. The whisper grew louder: "…who will remember you when you are gone?"

He began to feel unsteady on his feet, his mind spinning. Desperately, he reached out to the table for support, but his hand sank into the surface as if it were thick oil. His reflection reappeared, laughing, pitiless. Then it reached out and grabbed his wrist.

He screamed—not in fear, but in recognition. The reflection's grip was icy and soft, like the touch of something already forgotten. It pulled him down, inch by inch, until only his eyes remained above the table's sheen. His pupils dilated, reflecting all those he had humiliated.

And now, the last one: At first, nothing happened. He thought he had been spared—that by keeping still, praying, and not meeting their eyes, he had slipped through unnoticed. Relief swelled in him for a heartbeat, fragile and desperate.

Then the air shuddered. The walls groaned and split, peeling back like rotting flesh, revealing endless corridors of glass.

Behind each pane: scenes upon scenes, stacked into infinity—wars, abuse, executions, famines, screams. But amidst these horrors, he saw flashes of memory.

A man was bleeding out on the pavement in the underground walkway, and he had walked past. A woman sobbing behind a closed door, her bruises purple and yellow, begging him for help.

The teenage girl on the corner of the street, begging for food—eyes too big for her face.

He had walked away from all of them.

He tried to look away, but invisible hands reached out and grabbed his head, forcing him to watch. His eyelids blackened, then burned to ash, leaving only raw, wet sockets locked open. Blood streamed down his cheeks, but still, he saw—and remembered.

The glass screens began to crack and shatter, one by one. Each shard drove into him, embedding deep. With every cut, a life he could have changed.

He felt the woman's ribs crack under fists; he felt the teenage girl's hunger gnaw at his own gut; he felt the last, cold breath of the man he had ignored. Their pain coursed through him until he could no longer tell where they ended and where he began.

He screamed, but the sound that left him was not his own. It was theirs. Thousands of voices, each one accusing, each one familiar. The flood of horror accelerated, years of cruelty compressed into moments, all of it his fault, all of it his silence.

Then came the final cruelty. His body unravelled into smoke, but his eyes remained, two raw pits of sight without rest. They hung suspended before the endless corridors, condemned to watch every act he had ignored, every scream he had chosen not to hear.

When all else was gone, only the hollow gaze remained, seeing everything, saving no one, never able to look away.

Then, it was over. The room was empty. Only the adviser and the tall man remained. She rose, smoothed her suit jacket, and whispered, "Please send in the next group."

The man gave a curt nod, and together they vanished into the mist that had begun to form in the room.

Acknowledgement

I would like to express my deepest gratitude to my wife, Clare, whose constant support, encouragement, and belief in me have been my driving force throughout this journey. Her patience and understanding have kept me grounded, even during moments of self-doubt. To my family and friends, thank you for your unwavering support, whether through words of encouragement or simply being there when I needed a break from the writing. Your belief in me has been invaluable.A heartfelt thanks to my readers, your enthusiasm and curiosity fuel my passion to continue creating. I hope these stories resonate with you as deeply as they did with me while writing them.

I must acknowledge the inspiration drawn from the mysterious, the forgotten, and the unexplained. Without the haunting whispers of the unknown, this book would not have come to life. Thank you for allowing me to share these stories with you.

About the Author

Colin Reardon isn't a household name yet, but he hopes to be one day. He is passionate about everything paranormal and enjoys listening to others share their stories. Colin's interest in the paranormal began at a young age when his father used to talk about things he had witnessed, which only deepened Colin's fascination with things that go bump in the night.

Suffering from dyslexia, he found it hard to start his books and would often give up, but with the encouragement of his wife, Clare, he managed to complete his first book. Colin grew up in south-east London and now resides with his wife in Stockton-on-Tees.

Published in Collaboration with Noble Legacy Publishing

www.noblelegacypublishing.co.uk